I0640940

Firebrand

Firestorm

The Ancestors of Bjorn Esterday

Volume 16

Conversation Station

Wynter Sommers

Wynter Sommers

This work is registered with the UK Copyright Service, in accordance with the Copyright, Designs and Patents Act 1988 All rights reserved 284718040

USA Copyright © 2015 GJ dePillis
© 2015, TXu001966602 / 2015-05-08 and TXu001983965 / 2015-11-04

Library of Congress Control Number: 2020943167

Published by Pure Force Enterprises, Inc.
California, USA
Since 2002

INGRAM

INGRAM® Distribution

All rights reserved. All rights reserved. No part of this book may be used or reproduced by any means, graphic, electronic, or mechanical, including photocopying, recording, taping or by any information storage retrieval system without the written permission of the authors except in the case of brief quotations embodied in critical articles and reviews.
This novel is a work of fiction. Names, places, characters, and incidents are either the product of the author's imagination or, if real, are used fictitiously.

ISBN-13: 978-1-7184-0028-3
ISBN-10: 1-7184-0028-4

DEDICATION

To those who feel strongly about truth, justice, and the integrity of America; your honorable actions make us proud. To those who wonder if their daily choices matter; your small decisions impact generations to come.

To those everyday people who don't think they have what it takes; when you strive for extraordinary things, the impossible becomes reality.
Your dreams today become our future tomorrow.
Thank you for everything you do.

Bjorn Esterday
Was Not Born Yesterday
Series

Firebrand (15 Volumes+Conversation Station Book)
Edges (9 Stories +Conversation Station Book)
Gone (18 Stories + Conversation Station Book)

Bjorn EDGES Series
EDGES Book 1-Swift Encounter
EDGES Book 2-Rousing Attack
EDGES Book 3-One Foot Under
EDGES Book 4-Earthshake
EDGES Book 5-Broken String
EDGES Book 6-Key Witness
EDGES Book 7-Who is She?
EDGES Book 8-Vanish
EDGES Book 9-Chase or Die

Bjorn Series Alternate Reading Plan

1st	Edges Book 1		22nd	Gone Book 10
2nd	Edges Book 2		23rd	Firebrand Vol 9
3rd	Gone Book 1		24rd	Gone Book 11
4th	Firebrand Vol 1		25th	Firebrand Vol 10
5th	Edges Book 3		26th	Gone Book 12
6th	Firebrand Vol 2		27th	Gone Book 13
7th	Gone Book 2		28th	Firebrand Vol 11
8th	Gone Book 3		29th	Gone Book 14
9th	Firebrand Vol 3		30th	Firebrand Vol 12
10th	Gone Book 4		31st	Gone Book 15
11th	Firebrand Vol 4		32nd	Firebrand Vol 13
12th	Gone Book 5		33rd	Gone Book 16
13th	Gone Book 6		34th	Firebrand Vol 14
14th	Edges Book 4		35th	Gone Book 17
15th	Firebrand Vol 5		36th	Firebrand Vol15 (End)
16th	Gone Book 7		37th	Gone Book 18 (End)
17th	Firebrand Vol 6		38th	Edges Book 5
18th	Gone Book 8		39th	Edges Book 6
19th	Firebrand Vol 7		40th	Edges Book 7
20th	Gone Book 9		41st	Edges Book 8
21st	Firebrand Vol 8		42nd	Edges Book 9(End)

ACKNOWLEDGMENTS

We acknowledge those who actively build peace. We acknowledge all the selfless talent which contributed to creating meaningful tokens of consideration and sharing. We acknowledge that every person has a daily choice of right or wrong... and we thank you for choosing the right, good, honorable path filled with integrity because that is the difficult and brave path. Small choices today become lasting monuments of loving hope tomorrow.

CONTENTS

0 CHAPTER How To Use This Book

This book of conversation activities (or lesson plans) is intended to spark chatty discussion in a group setting, hence the title *Conversation Station.*

Each one of the fifteen (15) Firebrand volumes address a single theme, which shall be highlighted in this *Conversation Station,* book sixteen (16). Additional discussion topics of interest are addressed in the "Did You Know" section at the back of each individual volume. Every effort has been made to avoid duplication of the individual volume "Did You Know" section in this *Conversation Station* book to provide fresh material. There is also no answer key as there are no tests, per se. There are activities and ample discussion topics.

If you do not have a group, it is a great way to ignite a conversation with somebody else who has not been introduced to the series. These activities revolve around a core love of American History , adventure, and fondness for noble and chivalrous gallantry. .

There is one chapter dedicated to each of the volumes. You may consult the appropriate chapter in this book during and after your reading of one of the volumes. This book is intended to highlight an appreciation for Colonial American history as well as hone soft skills in the participants.

Understanding the motives of those in the 1700's and what drove them to fight for freedom is just as important a perspective to understand as is critical thinking to analyze character motives and how those lessons of yesteryear may still apply in modern times. Additionally, Group Conversation and empathy are valuable skills to develop.

Each volume contains a "vocabulary" section. Those have been collected and alphabetized in this Conversation Station.

Each chapter dedicated to a specific volume in Firebrand contains the following sections:

These sessions are structured to last approximately **60 minutes or more** depending on what you include in your group session. The group leader is able to modify the length of these flexible sessions from 20 minutes or longer by selecting or deselecting activities and group discussions. Each volume has three (3) structured activities, open ended questions for the group discussion, and an optional homework assignment. Vocabulary terms are collected from each volume and alphabetized at the end of this book.

Before starting any activity or assignment outside of the group setting, please verify with each participant that they are physically capable and willing to engage in the activity. If not, then skip that particular activity or the entire section, as is appropriate for your group.

These are the sub-sections pertaining to each volume in Firebrand:

1) **Assignments (Optional)** *from previous session:* Review the "after class" assignments you had assigned from the previous meeting. This could take longer if you ask the group participants to summarize to the group what they discovered. Depending on how complex the assignment was, the review process may take its own dedicated session. The optional assignment is at the end of each volume section. So when you start session covering volume 3, you are reviewing the optional assignment which had been assigned at the end of your session covering volume 2. You may also skip assigning any optional assignments at your discretion.
   ✓ Estimated Time: **5 minutes**

2) **Volume Theme.** This is a short theme which is highlighted in this set of conversation station activities. This may reference biblical verses which also support that theme. There might be an applicable scripture verse, which is appropriate for religious themed groups and can be skipped if the group is secular.
   ✓ Estimated time: **5 minutes**

3) **Chapters Referenced**: This is a list of the chapter titles in the volume which has been (or is being) read
   ✓ Estimated time: **3 minutes**

4) **<u>Structured Activities:</u>** These are suggestions for group activities. Structured activities may require some leader advance preparation.
   ✓ Estimated time: **24 minutes** (about 7 minutes per activity)

5) **<u>Objective Achieved:</u>** This summarizes what the participants should get out of this session. State the objective and ask the group if they think they have achieved this objective with the activities and announce you will start the group discussion.
   ✓ Estimated time: **3 minutes**

6) **<u>Group Conversation</u>**: These are open ended questions which spark conversation and dialogue in a group setting.
   ✓ Estimated time: **20 minutes** (this depends on how actively loquacious the group may be)

7) **<u>Assignments (Optional)</u>**: Suggested homework to be done solo or in a team. This new assignment is clarified right before this active session ends.
   ✓ Estimated time: **VARIED**. This takes place after the group has been dismissed and is optional. The amount of time it takes to complete this assignment will vary depending on if this is done solo or in a team setting. It also depends on how the group leader defines the output. For example, if it is to do research to have a conversation at the next meeting, the activity will take less time than if the group leader asks for a formally written paper with illustrations.

If you, as the group leader, plan to have a group discussion, there should be some ground rules.

11

Group Discussion RESORTS Rules:

RESORTS is an anagram to help you remember that the group should conduct conversations with: *Respect, Empathy, Sources, Opportunity, Rebuttal, Timing, Speculation.*

1) **RESPECT**: Profanity, vulgar comments, personal insults, patronizing attitudes, and lewd innuendo is NOT allowed. A dismissive attitude because a person may belong to some group you do not relate to is also frowned upon. The goal is to have a healthy active discussion and allow both friendly and shy participants the opportunity to freely share their ideas.

2) **EMPATHY**: Imagine yourself in the social class or profession of another...would that perspective change your opinion? Avoid blaming others for the opinions they hold.

3) **SOURCES**: If your comment is based on fact, please state the source. For example, "According to the book written by ____, I think the story really should have been this way___" If based on your personal opinion, please preface that by saying, "I think, in my own opinion, that the character should have chosen a different option instead of the one they took..."

4) **OPPORTUNITY**: Every person participating has the right and will have the opportunity to speak

5) **REBUTTAL**: If you are responding to the comment of another person in your group, please clarify that you have an issue with the concept shared, not the person who just shared the idea with which you

12

disagree.

6) **TIMING**: Each comment will be timed. Opinions on the comment just stated shall also be timed and the speaker will need to stop sharing when the moderator or group leader informs them when their time has run out.

7) **SPECULATION**: Speculation is permitted to anticipate what you think could happen to a certain character. This speculation may take you outside of the printed story line. Please try to confine your thoughts to be within the world of Firebrand during the 1770's. For example, introducing a space-ship alien attack may be considered "creative", but perhaps not a conversation trajectory everybody in the group could comment on. It is requested, therefore, that you confine your character speculations to still be within the appropriate time frame of Firebrand and how the actions of characters or events may impact the lives of future generations, for example in the EDGES or GONE series. Speculation about other participants in the group is discouraged as this may spark conflict and resentment and injured feelings within your group, preventing a productive conversation session.

◆🎕❋CHARACTERS❋🎕◆

♥ **Billy Dawes**- the carriage driver who befriends Silversmith.

♥ **Bryce Aiden** Tyler- Jane's Uncle Floyd's business partner

♥ **Button Gwinette** – the husband of Polly. Button defended his cabin during an attack to allow Polly, his wife, to escape. Button came to the Colonies to work in Georgia, where he owns land. When he married Polly, their land straddled the corners of Maryland Colony and Delaware Colony.

♥ **Eliza Lucas**- a young rugged girl who is experimenting with developing Indigo dye to counteract the red coats of the British. Her father has a rice plantation in the South Carolina colony and she believes Lady Sarah Wilson is not to be trusted.

♥ **Eunice Williams**, later *Marguerite Kanenstenhawi Arosen, of the Bear tribe.* Eunice married a man from the Wolf tribe. She was taken as a girl and raised as an Indian

♥ **Henry Mossop**- a former opera star who has fallen on hard times and now wants to make profit in another way. He left Ireland due to failed business and growing debt, and is now friends with Lady Sarah Wilson

♥ **Jane Hargreaves**- Once socially well positioned in England, her parents died, leaving all their wealth to the nearest married male relative, resulting in Jane becoming penniless save for a small allowance. She had to discharge an entire household of staff, save Silversmith. Uncle Floyd

14

sponsored Jane and Silversmith to voyage to the Colonies to live with him in Dover, Delaware.

♥ **Magistrate Karl Pinkney** - the official who works with Bryce to find out the truth. Karl has a brother who had to liquidate all his assets and send the proceeds to the King's Treasury. Karl is trying to find out why his brother was accused of a crime, yet cannot find out the nature of this crime.

♥ **Mr. Tweedbottom**- The tailor in town who is enamored with Jane Hargreaves

♥ **Mrs. Elizabeth Dunlap** – the wife of John Dunlap, Mrs. Dunlap allowed Polly to stay in their home in exchange for Bacoun (bacon).

♥ **Mr. John Dunlap**- He was born in Strabane, Pennsylvania then, after he apprenticed as a printer, set up shop in Philadelphia where he lives with his wife, Elizabeth.

♥ **Peter Timothy**- Son of Elizabeth Timothy, who wrote the book *Reflections on Courtship and Marriage* later attributed to Ben Franklin. He helps Silversmith and Billy Dawes to get closer to their goal.

♥ **Polly Mulhoolin**– the wife of Button Gwinette . They live in the undeveloped area West of New Castle, Delaware and North of Kent County and East of Cecil County in Maryland.

♥ **Sarah Wilson**- a woman of questionable past who has befriended Henry Mossop.

♥ **Silversmith**- Lady's maid and companion who travelled with Jane Hargreaves from England.

15

♥ **Simms**- Mr. and Mrs. Dunlap's butler

♥ **Susanna Wright**- an educated woman who organizes the secret meetings. The last of which occurred in a barn. She makes silk and helps her community in many capacities. She is from the Susquehanna River area in Pennsylvania.

♥ **TallMan** –the son of Eunice Williams; travelling medicine man.

♥ **Uncle Floyd Hargreaves** – Jane's Uncle who paid for both Jane and her maid, Silversmith's passage from England to his home in Dover, Delaware in the colonies in the New World

♥ **Witherspoon**- Jane's Uncle Floyd's butler

◆❀❋LOCATIONS❋❀◆

❶ Philadelphia: John & Elizabeth **Dunlap home**

❶ Philadelphia: The **State House** where the Declaration of Independence was signed.

❶ Philadelphia: **The Inn**

❶ Somewhere near or around Philadelphia: **Meeting Town**

❷ Maryland/Delaware Colonies: **Polly Mulhoolin & Button Gwinette** live in open wooded area straddling both the Maryland and Delaware colonies.

❸ Susquehanna, Pennsylvania: Where **Susanna Wright** is from

❹ Rising Sun, Maryland: Lady Sarah **Wilson's Estate**.

❺ Dover, Delaware: **Hargreaves Home** (Uncle Floyd lived there and invited and Jane and her lady's maid Silversmith to live with him there)

♣ South Carolina Colony: The colony from whence **Eliza Lucas** originally came. This does not appear on the map

♣ Canada: Where Tallman and his mother Eunice are from. This does not appear on the map

1st Volume Heed Warnings

Volume's Theme

Heed warnings

Proverbs 8:36 (The Voice Version) But heed my warning: the one who goes against me, will only hurt himself, for all who despise me are playing with fire and courting death.

Chapters Referenced

1 CHAPTER 01: (MARCH 1776) Run
2 CHAPTER 02: (FEB 1776) Getting Ready for Tea
3 CHAPTER 03: (MARCH 1776) Polly Ponders
4 CHAPTER 04: (FEB 1776) Tweedbottom Heads for Tea
5 CHAPTER 05: (MARCH 1776) Polly Recalls the Mundane Morning
6 CHAPTER 06: (FEB 1776) Tweedbottom Slows Down
7 CHAPTER 07: (MARCH 1776) Polly Sleeps On The Run

Preparation for Group

RESORTS conduct conversations with: *Respect, Empathy, Sources, Opportunity, Rebuttal, Timing, Speculation. See page 12.*

Group Leader Will Need:

✧ A place to write where the group can see, such as a chalk board, white board, or online virtual board.

✧ For activity #2, an image of a boat which would

have been used to travel from Europe to America, such as the Mayflower.

✧ A list of hobbies from the 18th century such as needlepoint or wood whittling.

This is a proposed cadence for conducting a structured session where the group host or instructor will keep the group members on track and usher the members from one section to the next with a specific output obtained by the end of the session.

Structured Activity 1

List everyday interactions with work, school, romance, or family communications where you have seen "red flags", which warn of something bad about to happen. In those situations, did you heed those warnings and avoid a harmful consequence, or did you ignore those warnings and feel the bite of a poor choice?

What happened when you warned others to avoid a red flag warning ?

Structured Activity 2

Imagine taking a boat journey from Europe to America. Write down or show examples of what you would pack. How much space on the ship would you have during the voyage? How long would the journey take?.

Structured Activity 3

Research common colonial hobbies, such as needlepoint, knitting, or wood whittling. Have you experience with any of these hobbies? Which would you want to learn? Can you present an example of one of these to the others in your group?

Objective Achieved: Understanding what life was like during voyages to the Colonies during 1770s.

Group Conversation

This is the proposed method of guiding a group in an open ended discussion. It could be different each time as the discussion may take various directions. The group host's responsibility is to remind the group when the time is coming to a close, and thank them for the group participation.

.

This is a set of questions. The trajectory of the conversation can take you in almost any direction. As the moderator or group leader and instructor, be prepared to remind the group that discussion should be respectful, fact-based, or if based on the speaker's opinion, is stated as such in advance, before sharing their ideas in this public forum.

In this forum, you can analyze character motivations and speculate about what might happen to the character even beyond the storyline in these Firebrand volumes. To ensure that no one speaker monopolizes the conversation, you may want to limit each comment to a specified duration of time, such as three to five minutes, and then allow other group members to respond.

1) With which character do you identify?

2) What do you think of the circumstances which caused Jane to leave England and travel to the Colonies?

3) Why do you think so many were willing to leave familiar European surroundings for an unknown New World?

4) What would need to happen to you in your life today to cause you to leave everything familiar to you and travel to a new land and decide to make it your home before you had even seen it?

5) Since the topic is heeding warnings or "red flags", have there been any warning signs you have noticed in your own experience? What were they and how did the warning signs affect you or the people you know?

To close this discussion, the group leader will thank the group members for their participation and remind them to pay attention to warning signs.

Assignments (Optional)

Optional assignments are suggested here for your participants to work on after the group discussion has ended. Encourage enthusiasm and proper research procedures. Invite your group to share their findings with each other at the next session, or you can have them submit their work directly to you, the group leader.

If they are dedicated to costuming- or dressing up as a specific character (cosplay), then encourage them to pick a character and sketch out what they think that character would look like. Then, they can return to the next session with some examples, such as pictures found during their research, or their own creation. Likewise, they can also demonstrate how they think hair was worn for women or men.

End of Conversation Station for this Volume 1

2ⁿᵈ Volume Perseverance

Volume's Theme

Perseverance

Romans 5:2-5 (New American Standard Bible NASB)...we exult in hope of the glory of God. 3 And not only this, but we also exult in our tribulations, knowing that tribulation brings about perseverance; 4 and perseverance, proven character; and proven character, hope; 5 and hope does not disappoint, because the love of God has been poured out within our hearts through the Holy Spirit who was given to us.

1 Timothy 6:11 (New American Standard Bible NASB)...pursue righteousness, godliness, faith, love, perseverance and gentleness.

Chapters Referenced

1 CHAPTER 08: (FEB 1776) Tea Time with Jane
2 CHAPTER 09: (MARCH 1776) Button Nabbed
3 CHAPTER 10: (FEB 1776) Did You Hear a Bang?
4 CHAPTER 11: (MARCH 1776) Button Looks Up
5 CHAPTER 12: (FEB 1776) Will You Investigate?

Preparation for Group

RESORTS conduct conversations with: *Respect, Empathy, Sources, Opportunity, Rebuttal, Timing, Speculation. See page 12.*

Group Leader Will Need:

✧ A way for group participants to write and share with others in the group.

✧ Examples of fashion from the 1700's for both men and women to compare to modern fashions.

✧ Examples of modern fashions

✧ List of "challenges" in everyday life during the 18th century.

✧ List of industries in the 18th century

This is a proposed cadence for conducting a structured session where the group host or instructor will keep the group members on track and usher the members from one section to the next with a specific output obtained by the end of the session.

Structured Activity 1

Write a list of difficult life situations from the 1770s and list if those same situations could occur today in modern times? What would be reasons to maintain perseverance through those difficult times in 1770? Are those the same reasons for perseverance today? Write a one sentence motto which is meaningful to you to remind yourself why you should NOT accept defeat and why you SHOULD keep going.

Structured Activity 2

Present the group with images of the fashions for men and for women in the 1770's. What elements were used in Europe, but were perhaps more difficult to obtain in the Colonies at that time? For example, whalebone was a material used for undergarments. Are those things used today? If not, is there a substitute material? The fashions in Colonial times may have needed a person to help you dress. Compare the manner of dressing back then to how a person dresses today. What is different and what is the same? What is your opinion about that?

Structured Activity 3

Write down the tools used in 1770 to manufacture objects, and would those same tools be used today? List the "tools" needed to make a batch of Indigo dye. How did Indigo differ from the red dye the British used to dye their "red coats"? What are the differences between the way red British dye was made versus blue Colonial dye? Do you think blue indigo dye bricks could have been used as currency in the Colonies? Why or why not?

Objective Achieved: Understand different aspects of persistence, perseverance, and manufacturing processes.

<u>Group Conversation</u>

This is the proposed method of guiding a group in an open ended discussion. It could be different each time as the discussion may take various directions. The group host's responsibility is to remind the group when the time is coming to a close, and thank them for the group participation.

.

This is a set of questions. The trajectory of the conversation can take you in almost any direction. As the moderator or group leader and instructor, be prepared to remind the group that discussion should be respectful, fact-based, or if based on the speaker's opinion, is stated as such in advance, before sharing their ideas in this public forum.

In this forum, you can analyze character motivations and speculate about what might happen to the character even beyond the storyline in these Firebrand volumes. To ensure that no one speaker monopolizes the conversation, you may want to limit each comment to a specified duration of time, such as three to five minutes, and then allow other group members to respond.

1) Under what circumstances would you persist versus give up?

2) What tools can be used in both 1770 and today to help somebody cope with defeat?

3) What inspires you to keep going? How do you inspire others to keep going?

4) How do you interpret a roadblock in your path? When is it a signal to take a different direction? When do you abandon your original course? When do you persist by breaking down barriers to forge ahead along that path undeterred?

5) Why do you think Jane wants to befriend Mr. Tweedbottom? What would he gain from this friendship, and what would she gain? Do either have anything to lose from this friendship?

6) Do you think others in this time period may have encountered what Button experienced? How do you think those events impacted pioneer life in early America?

7) Why is there a hesitancy to investigate Uncle Floyd? If Jane had a different status or had more wealth, would that make a difference? Have you felt dismissed or ignored because you were not at a social status which could demand attention? How was that overcome? What do you think Jane will do? Will she accept the final assessment of her Uncle, or will she do something else?

8) What sorts of characters are Billy Dawes, Silversmith and other servants in this story? Do you think a person in a "servant" role could affect anything significant? Do you think Billy would ever make a

strong impression? Why or why not?

9) Polly is faced with a surprise and feels unprepared. How have you reacted to startling situations where you were not only startled and unprepared, but had to respond quickly. What happened?

10) What do you think of the fashions of the 1770's for men and for women?

11) What do you think of the concept of homesteading? It is the concept that you will own 100 acres of land if you could simply build a home or cabin on the property? Would you move into the wilderness to claim your 100 acres?

To close this discussion, the group leader will thank group members for their participation, and remind them to remember the difference between a roadblock, signaling you to change direction and a roadblock, which requires persistence to break through that barrier.

<u>Assignments (Optional)</u>

Optional assignments are suggested here for your participants to work on after the group discussion has ended. Encourage enthusiasm and proper research procedures. Invite your group to share their findings with each other at the next session, or you can have them submit their work directly to you, the group leader.

.

For "perseverance", research examples of a real historical figure who persisted and overcame an obstacle. Or, find a modern person who struggled and overcame a barrier in current times.

Assume you were told you could have 100 acres of untamed natural property if you would build a home there. How would you go about making that property yours? Write a list of steps you would take to cultivate that land so that it produced something which could provide income for you and future generations.

End of Conversation Station for this Volume 2

3rd *Volume Encounters*

Volume's Theme

Encounters

Luke 14:31 (New American Standard Bible NASB) What king, when he sets out to meet another king in battle, will not first sit down and consider whether he is strong enough with ten thousand men to encounter the one coming against him with twenty thousand?

Chapters Referenced

1 CHAPTER 19: (MARCH 1776) Billy Dawes Stops the Carriage
2 CHAPTER 20: (MARCH 1776) Button and Day Three With the Tribe
3 CHAPTER 21: (MARCH 1776) BaCoun?
4 CHAPTER 22: (MARCH 1776) Button Runs
5 CHAPTER 23: (MARCH 1776) Polly and Jane Chat in the Carriage
6 CHAPTER 24: (MARCH 1776) The Farmer's Perspective.
7 CHAPTER 25: (MARCH 1776) Button Awakens In Farmer's Cart
8 CHAPTER 26: (1770-six years ago) Polly Meets Button at the Docks
9 CHAPTER 27: (1770) Polly At The Docks
10 CHAPTER 28: (1700) Polly on the Ship
11 CHAPTER 29: (1770-1774) After Polly Landed in the Colonies

Preparation for Group

RESORTS conduct conversations with: *Respect, Empathy, Sources, Opportunity, Rebuttal, Timing, Speculation. See page 12.*

Group Leader Will Need:

✧ Examples of modes of travel,

✧ Example of a ticket to go on a trip from the 1770s and from today,

✧ Prepare for a discussion on manners,

✧ List ways to identify a con man.

This is a proposed cadence for conducting a structured session where the group host or instructor will keep the group members on track and usher the members from one section to the next with a specific output obtained by the end of the session.

Structured Activity 1

List all the ways people would travel in 1770s. What was needed to prepare for those journeys? Compare that level of preparation to a similar journey today and discuss the differences.

Structured Activity 2

Compare an image of a ticket from the 1770s to a ticket today for a similar trip. What elements are on those tickets? Design a ticket to be used fifty years or more from today, and define what would change, and why.

Structured Activity 3

Evaluate the manners and protocols used when meeting a new person in different cultures. Write down the appropriate way a person should treat a stranger if that stranger is in distress.

How would the person rendering help make sure the distressed person was not a confidence trickster, conniving and trying to fool them? List ways a person may be fooled, and then list how that deceit should be uncovered and resolved.

Objective Achieved: Be friendly but wise when meeting new people during travels.

Group Conversation

This is the proposed method of guiding a group in an open ended discussion. It could be different each time as the discussion may take various directions. The group host's responsibility is to remind the group when the time is coming to a close, and thank them for the group participation.

This is a set of questions. The trajectory of the conversation can take you in almost any direction. As the moderator or group leader and instructor, be prepared to remind the group that discussion should be respectful, fact-based, or if based on the speaker's opinion, is stated as such in advance, before sharing their ideas in this public forum.

In this forum, you can analyze character motivations and speculate about what might happen to the character even beyond the storyline in these Firebrand volumes.

To ensure that no one speaker monopolizes the conversation, you may want to limit each comment to a specified duration of time, such as three to five minutes, and then allow other group members to respond.

1) Do you think Billy Dawes was smart when he stopped the carriage or do you think he should have just kept going? What would you have done as a driver?

2) Button feels trapped. Have you ever been in a situation where you felt there was no way out? How did you deal with it? What do you think will happen to Button?

3) We flash back in time to the 1770s where we see when Polly first met Button as she journeyed to the Colonies. How do you think the way they met influenced their relationship in 1776?

    a) What sort of foundation did it lay?

    b) How did the way they met affect their trust level in the relationship they have in 1776?

    c) What could you do today to start off a friendship to ensure a lasting relationship?

4) What sort of foundation do you think is needed to have a long lasting relationship?

    a) For a business relationship

    b) For a personal relationship? Would your techniques differ for a local friend as opposed to a relationship with a friend who lives very far away?

5) Describe a time when you planned a journey and then unexpectedly met some people along the way. How did that interaction make an impact on you reaching your final destination?

6) Some say life is a journey and that we need to appreciate each step as if those steps were the goal. Do you agree with that philosophy? Why or why not?

7) Have you intercepted another person on their own separate journey? What did you want them to remember about your encounter with them?

To close the group discussion, thank the group for their participation and offer them the option to do an activity after the group is dismissed. Remind them to pay attention to people they meet as they run their everyday routines as some of those encounters might become lasting friendships later on.

Assignments (Optional)

Optional assignments are suggested here for your participants to work on after the group discussion has ended. Encourage enthusiasm and proper research procedures. Invite your group to share their findings with each other at the next session, or you can have them submit their work directly to you, the group leader.

.Create a collage of images which show the different types of journeys to be taken. It could be a short trip or a long philosophical search. Now, imagine that the journey you depicted belongs to a total stranger. Mark the different places where you could make a contribution and write down what that contribution would be.

Imagine you are presented the chance to be introduced to somebody new. Clarify your contribution. How would you make that person's life a bit better after having encountered you?

End of Conversation Station for this Volume 3

4th Volume Seeking Truth

Volume's Theme

Seeking Truth

John 8:32 (21st Century King James Version) And ye shall know the truth, and the truth shall make you free.

.

Chapters Referenced

Preparation for Group

RESORTS conduct conversations with: *Respect, Empathy, Sources, Opportunity, Rebuttal, Timing, Speculation. See page 12.*

Group Leader Will Need:

✧ Images of face cosmetics for men and women in 1770s. Modern examples of cosmetics today.

✧ Examples of quality tailoring and poor tailoring in clothing in the 1770s and today.

✧ Examples of law enforcement in 1770 and today.

This is a proposed cadence for conducting a structured session where the group host or instructor will keep the group members on track and usher the members from one section to the next with a specific output obtained by the end of the session.

Structured Activity 1

Sketch or find pictures of face make-up in the 1700's for both men and women. Compare those to modern images.

Structured Activity 2

Mr. Tweedbottom is a tailor in this story. List ways you can examine a garment to determine if it was made by a quality tailor or not.

Structured Activity 3

Explain how the magistrate or other law-enforcement

officials operated in the Colonies. Compare that to how law enforcement works today. How is it the same or different? How do you think a suicide or murder would be investigated in 1770 versus today?

𝔒𝔟𝔧𝔢𝔠𝔱𝔦𝔳𝔢 𝔞𝔠𝔥𝔦𝔢𝔳𝔢𝔡 Compare how things were done in colonial times v today.

Group Conversation

This is the proposed method of guiding a group in an open ended discussion. It could be different each time as the discussion may take various directions. The group host's responsibility is to remind the group when the time is coming to a close, and thank them for the group participation.

.

This is a set of questions. The trajectory of the conversation can take you in almost any direction. As the moderator or group leader and instructor, be prepared to remind the group that discussion should be respectful, fact-based, or if based on the speaker's opinion, is stated as such in advance, before sharing their ideas in this public forum.

In this forum, you can analyze character motivations and speculate about what might happen to the character even beyond the storyline in these Firebrand volumes. To ensure that no one speaker monopolizes the conversation, you may want to limit each comment to a specified duration of time, such as three to five minutes, and then allow other group members to respond.

1) How do cosmetics and standards of beauty today compare to with those of the 18th century?

2) Do companies have a responsibility to avoid using dangerous substances when creating and selling items for public use? A cosmetic example would be white face paint, which was popular during the 1770's.

3) If you are seeking the truth, how could you discern if someone were lying to you?

4) Do you trust Mr. Tweedbottom? Why or why not?

5) Do you trust Mrs. Dunlap? Why or why not?

6) Do you trust Eliza Lucas? Why or why not?

7) Do you think that Bryce Aiden Tyler is pursuing a pointless hunt for truth? Why?

8) How would you comport yourself, and how would you dress, if summoned to dinner at the Wilson estate?

To close the group discussion, thank the group for their participation and offer them the option to do an activity after the group is dismissed.

Assignments (Optional)

Optional assignments are suggested here for your participants to work on after the group discussion has ended. Encourage enthusiasm and proper research procedures. Invite your group to share their findings with each other at the next session, or you can have them submit their work directly to you, the group leader.

List the ways in which those who lived in the colonies would verify something was true.

How did the Colonists interact with the King of England?

What would you do today to get a powerful authority figure to listen to your perspective, and then respectfully present your request to that authority?

End of Conversation Station for this Volume 4

5th *Volume Anticipation*

Volume's Theme

Anticipation

Psalm 119:148 American Standard Version (ASV) I anticipated the dawning of the morning... Mine eyes anticipated the night-watches, that I might meditate on thy word

Chapters Referenced

Preparation for Group

RESORTS conduct conversations with: *Respect, Empathy, Sources, Opportunity, Rebuttal, Timing, Speculation. See page 12.*

Group Leader Will Need:

✧ News headlines of current events (some true and some false)

✧ A list of social status classes

✧ A list of techniques to cope with stress

This is a proposed cadence for conducting a structured session where the group host or instructor will keep the group members on track and usher the members from one section to the next with a specific output obtained by the end of the session.

Structured Activity 1

If a human being is anxious or worried about an event versus a joyous occasion, the body responds differently. List the ways a body could respond physically if anticipating a stressor? What tools/ techniques could be used to cope with the stress? How are these responses the same or different from a human body which has undergone exercise?

Structured Activity 2

The group leader will present the group with a few statements about current events. Some are true and some will be false. Each group participant will list if the statement is either true or false. Next, list if you agree or disagree with the statement. In other words: Is the statement objectively factual? If it is, do you emotionally have an opinion about that statement? Why? What surprised you about this exercise? What pattern emerged with the group responses?

Structured Activity 3

Assume you are an average person who lives in the colonies. List all the stressful things which you would need to deal with. Do those stressful factors differ for each class of person? What would each socioeconomic group yearn for, hope for, crave, or anticipate?

Objective Achieved: Understand what triggers anticipation and how emotions can form opinions and influence actions.

Group Conversation

This is the proposed method of guiding a group in an open ended discussion. It could be different each time as the discussion may take various directions. The group host's responsibility is to remind the group when the time is coming to a close, and thank them for the group participation.

This is a set of questions. The trajectory of the conversation can take you in almost any direction. As the moderator or group leader and instructor, be prepared to remind the group that discussion should be respectful, fact-based, or if based on the speaker's opinion, is stated as such in advance, before sharing their ideas in this public forum.

In this forum, you can analyze character motivations and speculate about what might happen to the character even beyond the storyline in these Firebrand volumes. To ensure that no one speaker monopolizes the conversation, you may want to limit each comment to a specified duration of time, such as three to five minutes, and then allow other group members to respond.

1) List the elements of anticipation, in your opinion

2) How does anticipation differ from other emotions like anger, frustration. excitement, and hope?

3) If Anticipation and hope are intertwined, what tips can you give to somebody who is hopeful and wants a good outcome but is impatient? How would you advise them?

4) Bryce and Witherspoon have narrowed down the list of what could have happened with Uncle Floyd. Are they wasting their time? Why or why not?

5) Bacon (Bacoun) was used as payment for Polly. If you were the Dunlaps, would you have insisted on money instead of a bartered good? Why or why not?

6) Explain why bacon or any other good was used for bartering? What do you think happened to the value of currency in those colonies with the governmental power shifting around? What product was considered a wise investment to hold value?

6) Button is exhausted from trying to escape. He just wanted to live his life in peace, but was forced from his home. Now, should Button trust this farmer? What would you do if you were the farmer? What if you were Button?

To close the group discussion, thank the group for their participation and offer them the option to do an activity after the group is dismissed. Remind your group members to examine their own hopes and dreams. How can they develop the empathetic skill to understand what motivates others to yearn and anticipate?

Assignments (Optional)

Optional assignments are suggested here for your participants to work on after the group discussion has ended. Encourage enthusiasm and proper research procedures. Invite your group to share their findings with each other at the next session, or you can have them submit their work directly to you, the group leader.

Research data from psychology sources regarding triggering various emotions.

How does the body physically respond when experiencing joy, fear, anticipation, stress, relaxation, etc.?

If a person has suffered a traumatic event, what is the trigger which causes them to react? What techniques or tools could be used to help that person process the trigger differently? What could help them cope and heal from the traumatic experience?

End of Conversation Station for this Volume 5

6ᵗʰ Volume Seek and Find

Volume's Theme

Seek and Find

Matthew 6:33(American Standard Version)But seek ye first his kingdom, and his righteousness; and all these things shall be added unto you.

Chapters Referenced

Preparation for Group

RESORTS conduct conversations with: *Respect, Empathy, Sources, Opportunity, Rebuttal, Timing, Speculation. See page 12.*

Group Leader Will Need:

✧ List of steps for conducting basic research

✧ Written set of proper dinner table manners

✧ List of steps for a negotiation: Prepare, Information Exchange, Bargain, Conclude, Execute.

This is a proposed cadence for conducting a structured session where the group host or instructor will keep the group members on track and usher the members from one section to the next with a specific output obtained by the end of the session.

Structured Activity 1

List all the lessons you learned when investigating and hunting down the truth. How would you convey those lessons to another if you were a mentor and they were a protege?

Structured Activity 2

Review the dynamics of a group dinner. Some say deals are made at the dinner table, and contracts are signed in the conference room. This means that a social setting fosters the agreement between two parties but the formal contract is signed in the office the next business day. Do you agree with that statement? List why or why not.

Structured Activity 3

List the elements needed for a successful negotiation in 1770 versus a negotiation today. How were emotions of large groups of people influenced then compared to now?

> Hint: Some components of negotiation include Prepare, Information Exchange, Bargain, Conclude, Execute agreed upon terms

> Hint: Some marketing techniques or propaganda messages are used to sway the opinion of large groups of people. What is one way to do this?

Objective Achieved: Understand how negotiations were conducted in the 1770s.

Group Conversation

This is the proposed method of guiding a group in an open ended discussion. It could be different each time as the discussion may take various directions. The group host's responsibility is to remind the group when the time is coming to a close, and thank them for the group participation.

.

This is a set of questions. The trajectory of the conversation can take you in almost any direction. As the moderator or group leader and instructor, be prepared to remind the group that discussion should be respectful, fact-based, or if based on the speaker's opinion, is stated as such in advance, before sharing their ideas in this public forum.

In this forum, you can analyze character motivations and speculate about what might happen to the character even beyond the storyline in these Firebrand volumes. To ensure that no one speaker monopolizes the conversation, you may want to limit each comment to a specified duration of time, such as three to five minutes, and then allow other group members to respond.

1) In Jane's efforts to discover the truth, what do you think she is learning at the Wilson estate? Is it useful?

2) Why do the men and women separate after dinner during the 1700s? Is that practiced today after a group dinner concludes? Why or why not?

3) What do you think Button is really seeking? What do you think he will eventually find? Why do you think that?

4) Jane and Tweedbottom seem to have altered the tone of their friendship. Why did that happen? What caused it? Do you agree with Jane's reaction or not? Why?

5) When a new piece of evidence is discovered, does that change anything? Why or why not?

6) In volume six, we see that three months after the raid, there is a meeting. What is the goal of this meeting? What do you think the outcome will be?

7) If you wanted to find the truth about something, how have you gone about seeking, finding, and verifying the truth? What lessons would you share with others?

To close the group discussion, thank the group for their participation and offer them the option to do an activity after the group is dismissed.

Assignments (Optional)

Optional assignments are suggested here for your participants to work on after the group discussion has ended. Encourage enthusiasm and proper research procedures. Invite your group to share their findings with each other at the next session, or you can have them submit their work directly to you, the group leader.

Find a reference (for example, from an old law book) from England and also one from the Colonies during the 1770s to see if there were any consequences for lying to the court.

Compare that to the penalty today for lying in court. What is your opinion on the similarities or differences between the same infraction, but in two different time periods.

What does it tell you about which character values are important throughout the centuries?

End of Conversation Station for this Volume 6

9ᵗʰ Volume Secrets

Volume's Theme

Secrets

Psalm 91 (Contemporary English Version) The Lord Is My Fortress. Live under the protection of God Most High and stay in the shadow of God All-Powerful. Then you will say to the Lord, "You are my fortress, my place of safety; you are my God, and I trust you." The Lord will keep you safe from secret traps and deadly diseases. ...

Chapters Referenced

Preparation for Group

RESORTS conduct conversations with: *Respect, Empathy, Sources, Opportunity, Rebuttal, Timing, Speculation. See page 12.*

Group Leader Will Need:

✧ List of social class structure in the 1700s

✧ Recipe for invisible ink, which you either prepared for an in-person meeting or ask your participants to make from household ingredients in advance.

✧ Have a "mask" (decoder page), which is a piece of paper with holes cut out to reveal the real message when that "mask" is laid on top of another paper which contains the writing hiding in the coded message.

This is a proposed cadence for conducting a structured session where the group host or instructor will keep the group members on track and usher the members from one section to the next with a specific output obtained by the end of the session.

Structured Activity 1

Secret ink was used in Colonial times to pass messages along. Make some invisible ink and create your own secret message. What is the best way to reveal the message?

Structured Activity 2

Some messages were decoded with a mask, or another paper with holes cut out of it which lay on top of the original letter. Create a "mask" by which to decode a message.

Structured Activity 3

Research individuals who were later revealed to be spies in the 1700s to the end of the Revolutionary war. The Revolutionary war was from April 19, 1775 – September 3, 1783. Why do you think these people became spies?

Objective Achieved Learn about covert operation techniques which occurred in Colonial times.

Group members should understand the level of work needed to communicate in order to win the Revolutionary War.

Group Conversation

This is the proposed method of guiding a group in an open ended discussion. It could be different each time as the discussion may take various directions. The group host's responsibility is to remind the group when the time is coming to a close, and thank them for the group participation.

.

This is a set of questions. The trajectory of the conversation can take you in almost any direction. As the moderator or group leader and instructor, be prepared to remind the group that discussion should be respectful, fact-based, or if based on the speaker's opinion, is stated as such in advance, before sharing their ideas in this public forum.

In this forum, you can analyze character motivations and speculate about what might happen to the character even beyond the storyline in these Firebrand volumes. To ensure that no one speaker monopolizes the conversation, you may want to limit each comment to a specified duration of time, such as three to five minutes, and then allow other group members to respond.

1) What does the magistrate's brother say? Have you ever been briefly introduced to a new acquaintance, who asked you for insight on a topic? Did you shed light and provide understanding about a situation?

2) What is the book which Billy Dawes accidentally grabs? Why does it cause Silversmith to blush?

Hint: A sample might be in the back of the final 15th book in this Firebrand series.

3) What prompts Button to speak up at the barn?

Have you ever wanted to stay quiet but then something triggered you to be bold? What was that trigger?

4) What was Mrs. Dunlap's secret? Have you ever had a secret which was really a lesson learned from somebody else? What was that valuable lesson?

5) What was life like for printers in the 1770s in Colonial America? Were there certain topics a woman could or should not publish? Why was reputation so valuable in those days and is it just as valuable today?

6) Do you agree with how Jane interacted with Mr. Tweedbottom? Why or why not?

7) What are your thoughts on the value of indigo blocks of dye? Have you heard of the term "blue gold" (Indigo dye bricks used as currency)?

8) GROUP LEADER: Read this passage aloud to the group and get member feedback about the following:

   a) *Mrs. Elizabeth Timothy was also the first woman news printer. She ran the South Carolina Gazette. It was suspected she and Mrs. Franklin discussed the proper way to have a marriage. It was further supposed that Mrs. Timothy typeset and printed up their thoughts in a small book reflecting on marriage and courtship.*

   b) *Due to the sensitive nature of the book, it was not proper at the time for either lady, especially a widow, to put her name to such a topic. Thus, it is suspected that Mr. Franklin was able to put* *his name on the manuscript so both his wife and his wife's friend could share and profit from the sale of **"Reflections on Courtship and Marriage"** back in 1746. This could be why the work is attribute to Mr. Benjamin Franklin and not Mrs. Deborah Franklin and her friend Mrs. Elizabeth Timothy.*

c) Group Leader: If any participant asks for more details about the **"Reflections on Courtship and Marriage"** point out that the full text is in the DID YOU KNOW section of Firebrand volume 15.

To close the group discussion, thank the group for their participation and offer them the option to do an activity after the group is dismissed. Remind participants that keeping a confidence is respected and appreciated. Be a trustworthy character.

Assignments (Optional)

Optional assignments are suggested here for your participants to work on after the group discussion has ended.

Encourage enthusiasm and proper research

procedures. Invite your group to share their findings with each other at the next session, or you can have them submit their work directly to you, the group leader.

Examine the social dynamics of class structure in the 1700s in England and in the Colonies.

How would that class-structure affect your modern world if it was brought back today? Would it change your daily routine?

How would it alter your relationships?

How did that class-structure influence covert operations and spying during Colonial times?

Which class controlled the communication channels of spy rings?

End of Conversation Station for this Volume 7

8ᵗʰ Volume Outrage

Volume's Theme

Outrage

Psalm 78:49 (New King James Version) He cast on them the fierceness of his anger, wrath, indignation, and trouble by sending angels of destruction among them. .

Chapters Referenced

1 CHAPTER 70: (JUNE 1776) Polly Meets New Friends
2 CHAPTER 71: (1704) Eunice's Story
3 CHAPTER 72: (1705) Catholic Mohawks
4 CHAPTER 73: (JUNE 1776) Reaction to Eunice Adoption
5 CHAPTER 74: (JUNE 1776) The Barn Is Still Talking
6 CHAPTER 75: (JUNE 1776) Eunice and TallMan At the Dunlap's Door
7 CHAPTER 76: (JUNE 1776) At Mrs. Dunlap's Front Door
8 CHAPTER 77: (JUNE 1776) Peter Timothy Leads Them To The Barn
9 CHAPTER 78: (June 1776) 1697 Story of Hannah
10 CHAPTER 79: (June 1776) 1697 The English Way vs. The French Way
11 CHAPTER 80: (JUNE 1776) Fuming By The Haystack

Preparation for Group

RESORTS conduct conversations with: *Respect, Empathy, Sources, Opportunity, Rebuttal, Timing, Speculation. See page 12.*

Group Leader Will Need:

✧ List contact information about local animal adoption, a wildlife refuge, or animal shelter, such as "the pound"

✧ List contact information for local adoption agencies or libraries where adoption processes are available for the participants

✧ Examples of adoption depicted in literature

This is a proposed cadence for conducting a structured session where the group host or instructor will keep the group members on track and usher the members from one section to the next with a specific output obtained by the end of the session.

Structured Activity 1

Go to your local animal shelter or dog-training school and ask about their adoption policy. Are there any wildlife adoption establishments in the area? What is the process to rehabilitate an injured wild animal? Is helping an injured wild animal considered "adoption"?

Structured Activity 2

Look up your local children's home and ask about their foster or adoption policy.

Note: "children's home" is the term to reference a place where children are housed and educated while their parents are unavailable to parent them. For example, the parents may be incarcerated for a duration of time.

Compare all the forms of animal and human adoption and see what they have in common and what are their differences. How does modern human adoption differ from the way Eunice was taken in by her adopted family?

Structured Activity 3

Discuss works of literature which highlight an adopted individual (human or non-human) and analyze what elements made that story interesting. The story could be in any format: book, comic book, manga, cartoon animation, graphic novel, movie, radio theater, etc?

Objective Achieved Empathize with the perspective of an adoptee and understand the full adoption process.

Group Conversation

This is the proposed method of guiding a group in an open ended discussion. It could be different each time as the discussion may take various directions. The group host's responsibility is to remind the group when the time is coming to a close, and thank them for the group participation.

This is a set of questions. The trajectory of the conversation can take you in almost any direction. As the moderator or group leader and instructor, be prepared to remind the group that discussion should be respectful, fact-based, or if based on the speaker's opinion, is stated as such in advance, before sharing their ideas in this public forum.

In this forum, you can analyze character motivations and speculate about what might happen to the character even beyond the storyline in these Firebrand volumes. To ensure that no one speaker monopolizes the conversation, you may want to limit each comment to a specified duration of time, such as three to five minutes, and then allow other group members to respond.

1) Does learning the story of TallMan's mother from 1704 give you a different perspective into what influences made him the man he is in 1776?

2) What childhood influences made you who you are today? If you experienced a memorable event, does that color how you see events today? How?

3) What is your opinion about why some Mohawks adopted the Catholic religion?

4) What do you think can be accomplished with these secret meetings in the barn? How do you think coordination of many people can influence an established power base? Share modern-day examples.

5) Do you think that those with evil selfish motives eventually "get their comeuppance", or do they "get away with it"? What examples justify your opinion?

6) Have you ever had to move to a new place and felt as if you did not have much say in that decision to relocate? How did you cope with that transition? How did you make the best of it or did you fight it and let everybody around you know how bad a decision this was?

7) Think about Eunice's story. What did she do to cope with her situation? Do you think her understanding of two cultures made her able to think of a peaceful way for two cultures to interact? Why?

8) What steps would you take to adapt to a new location? How would you learn the geography and environment, including local customs, and how would you start making human connections so this could become your new home?

To close the group discussion, thank the group for their participation and offer them the option to do an activity after the group is dismissed. Remind them that outrage over an injustice is understandable but that emotion must convert into actionable steps to make the world a better place.

Assignments (Optional)

Optional assignments are suggested here for your participants to work on after the group discussion has ended. Encourage enthusiasm and proper research procedures. Invite your group to share their findings with each other at the next session, or you can have them submit their work directly to you, the group leader.

Research: How did different cultures in the 1700s make peace and war with other cultures?

What events caused war? What events resulted in peace?

What incentives caused a tribe to be hired-out by a foreign government to execute attacks on certain populations and do another government's "hit job", be hired mercenaries, or do their other "dirty work"?

What industries paid well during Colonial times?

Does making a profit indicate that a certain business will thrive and be successful, even if it is moral or immoral? Can you name some companies which are over 50 to 100 years old? Why did they last?

End of Conversation Station for this Volume 8

9ᵗʰ Volume Onward

Volume's Theme

Onward

Jeremiah 29:11 (Common English Bible) I know the plans I have in mind for you, declares the Lord; they are plans for peace, not disaster, to give you a future filled with hope.

.

Chapters Referenced

1 CHAPTER 81: (JUNE 1776) Mrs. Dunlap Gets a Letter
2 CHAPTER 82: (JUNE 1776) Silversmith Sees Stable Boys returning too fast.
3 CHAPTER 83: (JUNE 1776) Where is Jane?
4 CHAPTER 84: (JUNE 1776) Button at the end of the Barn meeting
5 CHAPTER 85: (JUNE 1776) Jane's Carriage trip
6 CHAPTER 86: (MAY 1776) Reading The Diary- What to Share with Magistrate
7 CHAPTER 87: (JUNE 1776) Later At Jane's Hired Carriage

Preparation for Group

RESORTS conduct conversations with: *Respect, Empathy, Sources, Opportunity, Rebuttal, Timing, Speculation. See page 12.*

Group Leader Will Need:

✧ Images of household items from modern and colonial times.

✧ List of famous Colonial people

This is a proposed cadence for conducting a structured session where the group host or instructor will keep the group members on track and usher the members from one section to the next with a specific output obtained by the end of the session.

Structured Activity 1

List famous men and women from Colonial times. What made some more memorable than others?

Structured Activity 2

Write the sacrifice you would be willing to make to ensure your home remained free from tyranny? How do tyranny, monarchy, and democracy differ?

Structured Activity 3

Assemble a collage of everyday items found in the home during colonial times. What is the same and what has become modernized? Could you live in a home using only Colonial-era objects?

Objective Achieved: Be able to describe some elements of everyday life during Colonial times. Include some of their challenges.

Group Conversation

This is the proposed method of guiding a group in an open ended discussion. It could be different each time as the discussion may take various directions. The group host's responsibility is to remind the group when the time is coming to a close, and thank them for the group participation.

This is a set of questions. The trajectory of the conversation can take you in almost any direction. As the moderator or group leader and instructor, be prepared to remind the group that discussion should be respectful, fact-based, or if based on the speaker's opinion, is stated as such in advance, before sharing their ideas in this public forum.

In this forum, you can analyze character motivations and speculate about what might happen to the character even beyond the storyline in these Firebrand volumes. To ensure that no one speaker monopolizes the conversation, you may want to limit each comment to a specified duration of time, such as three to five minutes, and then allow other group members to respond.

1) Document a plan for your future? Where might you be in five years and 15 years?

2) Five years ago, did you think you would be where you are today? If you did not follow your plan, what "bumps in the road" made you change course? How do you deal with unexpected events which force you to alter your plans?

3) What do you think happened to Jane?

4) Jane would not be in this situation unless she was hunting for the truth about her Uncle. Was she right or wrong to follow this path?

5) What might be written in the diary which could alter the outcome of the investigation?

6) Do you agree or disagree with the motivations of Billie Dawes, the driver? Why?

To close the group discussion, thank the group for their participation and offer them the option to do an activity after the group is dismissed.

Remind them that they must forge onward despite a gloomy surrounding. Do not be discouraged. Summon up the last vestiges of strength to make even the smallest baby-step forward. Moving forward, no matter how tiny the increment, is still progress.

Assignments (Optional)

Optional assignments are suggested here for your participants to work on after the group discussion has ended. Encourage enthusiasm and proper research procedures. Invite your group to share their findings with each other at the next session, or you can have them submit their work directly to you, the group leader.

Understand what was needed to set up a home in the Colonies, and then select a political side right before the Revolutionary War started.

Write how you would you have reacted if you lived in one of the thirteen Colonies during that time? If both sides tried to recruit you, then how would you decide which side to defend and fight for?

End of Conversation Station for this Volume 9

10ᵗʰ Volume Suspicion

Volume's Theme

Suspicion

Deuteronomy 20:3 (King James Version)... ye approach this day unto battle against your enemies: let not your hearts faint, fear not, and do not tremble, neither be ye terrified because of them...

Chapters Referenced

Preparation for Group

RESORTS conduct conversations with: *Respect, Empathy, Sources, Opportunity, Rebuttal, Timing, Speculation. See page 12.*

Group Leader Will Need:

✧ Images of historic figures on horses

✧ Images of animals used in war (dogs, ox, etc.)

✧ List of animals used for PTSD therapy

✧ Etymology Dictionary

✧ Ability to display and update a list which is visible to the entire group

This is a proposed cadence for conducting a structured session where the group host or instructor will keep the group members on track and usher the members from one section to the next with a specific output obtained by the end of the session.

Structured Activity 1

Historical statues of men who won battles are often depicted astride a horse. What role do you think horses played in Colonial times? Write a list of animals which were vital during battle and what function they played.

Structured Activity 2

List animals which can be used to aid somebody who has suffered from trauma. Horses, dogs, parrots, carrier pigeons? Research examples of each animal and discuss how to train them to alleviate fears in somebody who has suffered a serious shock (PTSD= Post Traumatic Stress Disorder or "shell shock")

Structured Activity 3

List ways you would prepare in the event of an enemy attack (recall what happened in Firebrand Volume 10 Chapter 7 CHAPTER 94: (JUNE 1776) The King's Men Descend. Susanna grabs Button) How would you hold a meeting which might get disbanded by the opposition, and how would you react?

Objective achieved Compare how animals were used in battle in Colonial times and how they are used in conflicts today. Learn preparation tactics for covert meetings.

Group Conversation

This is the proposed method of guiding a group in an open ended discussion. It could be different each time as the discussion may take various directions. The group host's responsibility is to remind the group when the time is coming to a close, and thank them for the group participation.

This is a set of questions. The trajectory of the conversation can take you in almost any direction. As the moderator or group leader and instructor, be prepared to remind the group that discussion should be respectful, fact-based, or if based on the speaker's opinion, is stated as such in advance, before sharing their ideas in this public forum.

In this forum, you can analyze character motivations and speculate about what might happen to the character even beyond the storyline in these Firebrand volumes. To ensure that no one speaker monopolizes the conversation, you may want to limit each comment to a specified duration of time, such as three to five minutes, and then allow other group members to respond.

1) How do you cope with a situation which alarms you or causes you fear?

2) What have you done to help soothe others when they seem afraid?

3) What lessons can you learn from being in a situation that seems impossible and overwhelming? How do you handle situations when the odds are against you?

4) Have you experienced a narrow escape in your life? What lesson did you learn from that? How did you prepare for the adverse situation?

5) Silversmith and Billy seem to have low level social positions as servants, but they play a vital part in this story and are the ones who link together Peter Timothy with the the key characters. What contributions do you think you could make in your life today, which seem small, but may become consequential?

6) If you were Button in Firebrand, how would you handle the events he has had to endure?

Thank the group for their participation and offer them the option to do an activity after the group is dismissed.

Assignments (Optional)

Optional assignments are suggested here for your participants to work on after the group discussion has ended. Encourage enthusiasm and proper research procedures. Invite your group to share their findings with each other at the next session, or you can have them submit their work directly to you, the group leader.

List the triggers you have which cause you anxiety and fear. Then list a way to cope with those triggers when you recognize them. Keep the list with you in case you experience a trigger and need to address it quickly.

Include ways to handle the following:

✧ How to deal with rejection

✧ How to deal with a negative comment about your idea or work product

✧ How to avoid extreme situations which may evoke stress

✧ How to handle nightmares

✧ How to take a past trauma and analyze it objectively

✧ Write three words which have been in use for over 100 years. Look up the entomological journey of these words to determine how the meaning has changed over time.

EXAMPLE:

The word "shock" has been in use since the 1560's. It was originally defined as a "violent encounter of armed forces or a pair of warriors". Some feel this may have come from a French military term *"choc"*, which could be translated as "violet attack" or from the French *"choquer"* to strike against. In the Colonies, there was a large population of Dutch and Germans, so the word could have also been influenced by the German s*coc*, which means "jolt" Around 1610, the meaning became "a sudden blow". In 1705, the definition also included "a sudden and disturbing impression on the mind", or "feeling of being (mentally) shocked." As time progressed, language added different dimensions to the meaning of "shock".

End of Conversation Station for this Volume 10

11ᵗʰ Volume Wicked Schemes

Volume's Theme

Wicked Schemes

Psalm 73:7 (Good News Translation) Their hearts pour out evil, and their minds are busy with wicked schemes.

Chapters Referenced

1 CHAPTER 102: (JULY 1 1776) Spy Silversmith Through the Coffee Shop Window as the Chase ensues?
2 CHAPTER 103: (JULY 1 1776) Bryce Corners Henry Mossop
3 CHAPTER 104: (JULY 2 1776) Heading to the docks to find him
4 CHAPTER 105: (JULY 2 1776) Kidnapped, again!
5 CHAPTER 106: (JULY 2, 1776) Button and The Good Samaritan
6 CHAPTER 107: (JULY 2 1776) Primo Uomo Defense
7 CHAPTER 108: (JULY 2 1776) The women and the Irish Sailor
8 CHAPTER 109: (JULY 2, 2015) The Women and Spot the Figure
9 CHAPTER 110: (JULY 2, 2015) the Sailor Returns
10 CHAPTER 111: (JULY 2, 1776) Eliza Shouts Orders
11 CHAPTER 112: (JULY 2, 1776): Jane finds Eliza, Moments Before the Splash
12 CHAPTER 113: (JULY 2 1776) Polly's Settles in the Inn

Preparation for Group

RESORTS conduct conversations with: *Respect, Empathy, Sources, Opportunity, Rebuttal, Timing, Speculation. See page 12.*

Group Leader Will Need:

✧ List of social class structure in England and America to compare

This is a proposed cadence for conducting a structured session where the group host or instructor will keep the group members on track and usher the members from one section to the next with a specific output obtained by the end of the session.

Structured Activity 1

Write a list of social classes in England during the 1770s and in England today.

Write a list of what you believe the social classes were in the Colonies during the 1770s. Find documentation to show socioeconomic classes in the United States of America today.

What differences do you observe?

Structured Activity 2

Examine the social class lists and see where someone you know would fit if they were residing in England, or if they were residing in the Colonies during the 1770s. What would life be like for that person?

Which country would give that individual more opportunity for a comfortable life? Compare the two modern day social structures of England and the United States of America. Share which country provides more social mobility to allow for personal success? Why do you think that is?

Structured Activity 3

Pretend you have your own country. Structure an ideal class system and explain what role each class would serve in your society.

Objective Achieved Understand how social classes permit and prevent social mobility and opportunity.

Group Conversation

This is the proposed method of guiding a group in an open ended discussion. It could be different each time as the discussion may take various directions. The group host's responsibility is to remind the group when the time is coming to a close, and thank them for the group participation.

.

This is a set of questions. The trajectory of the conversation can take you in almost any direction. As the moderator or group leader and instructor, be prepared to remind the group that discussion should be respectful, fact-based, or if based on the speaker's opinion, is stated as such in advance, before sharing their ideas in this public forum.

In this forum, you can analyze character motivations and speculate about what might happen to the character even beyond the storyline in these Firebrand volumes. To ensure that no one speaker monopolizes the conversation, you may want to limit each comment to a specified duration of time, such as three to five minutes, and then allow other group members to respond.

1) Why do you think coffee shops or tea shops were a popular place to discuss ideas and conduct business? Has that practice changed from the 1770s versus today?

2) Why would strangers who do not know Button head to the docks to try and find a man they never met? What factors would drive you to help another person?

3) What do you think of the Irish sailors? What motivates them to live as they do? Could you see yourself as a Colonial sailor in 1776?

4) Some wicked people seem to get away with their

crimes, but most evil schemes eventually implode. What is your opinion on good versus evil in the world? How should good be strengthened to avoid villainy from gaining control?

5) The women, although searching for one thing, happen upon a great number of people who are in need of their service. Would you endanger your own safety to render aid to a group of strangers in need? Why or why not?

6) Do you agree with what the women did? Where do you think this act will get them, and is it worth it?

7) Polly has her own struggles which she feels she must handle by herself. She is in a new situation which is less than ideal. How would you handle the circumstances if you were in Polly's position?

To close the group discussion, thank the group for their participation and offer them the option to do an activity after the group is dismissed.

Remind the group that a crime is a crime. When tempted to commit a crime, stop and consider the consequences. Then, do not do it. Always choose the path of integrity and honor.

Assignments (Optional)

Optional assignments are suggested here for your participants to work on after the group discussion has ended. Encourage enthusiasm and proper research procedures. Invite your group to share their findings with each other at the next session, or you can have them submit their work directly to you, the group leader.

Option 1:

List common crimes in the 1700s and their punishments. How do those punishments compare with modern law enforcement?

Option 2:

Draw a chart showing how the social classes relate to each other. It may be challenging to locate documentation for social class structure in the Colonies and in England prior to the 1800s, so feel free to review the social class lists on the next few pages.

Option 3:

Those who settled in the Colonies of America tried to structure a new social order. If a person was born into a class in England, with its rigid European class system, they remained in that class until they died. If,

84

however, they moved to the Colonies, how might they take advantage of the unstructured social classes in the Colonies to earn a better living (better social mobility)? Did that have a positive or negative effect on the American culture?

Option 4

Instructions:

The next few pages will present several lists of British social classes throughout time.

Review all the lists and then write your observations regarding any patterns you see as class structure changed over time.

Why did society want to classify their people?

18th Century Class Structure (one perspective)

Royalty: These are the immediate family of whoever holds the crown along with their spouse and children.

Peerage: Dukes, marquesses, earls, viscounts, or barons were people to whom the crown granted a title which could be passed on to future generations (hereditary titles). During the reigns of George I and George II, there were 170 peers. These were the elites who set the cultural tone of society and dominated power positions in government. They could sit in the House of Lords. Many of these MPs (Members of Parliament) in the House of Commons owned land. They were considered land owners. About 300 families owned estates ranging from 10,000 to 20,000 acres.

Merchants: These were people in businesses, such as industry and trade. This would include brewing, banking, textiles, etc. Those who belong to the merchant class are from families who could earn enough money from the business transactions during their lifetime where they could purchase estate homes, country villas, or town houses.

Tradesmen: These people are boutique owners, which include shops, notions (sewing shop), toys, and jewelry stores. Napoleon Bonaparte might have referred to Britain as a nation of shopkeepers.

Professionals, Artisans and Day laborers: Importing became a profession for those who wanted sell porcelain china, armchairs, fancy mirrors, newspapers, and manufactured toys.

Middle income: This group did not start to grow until the mid 1700's when opportunities opened up in law, teaching, medicine, banking, and luxury industries which catered to the wealthy.

Middle class: These are people who would be small business owners or hold jobs where they can pay for their own housing and support a family.

Working class: This group was comprised of unskilled

and semi-skilled labor. There were also some professions which were skilled, yet they were considered the upper portion of the working class and not quite lower-middle class.

Underclass - these are people who are chronically unemployed.

19th Century Class Structure (one perspective) This understanding is comprised from many sources including, *A Treatise of the Wealth, Power, and Resources of the British Empire, in Every Quarter of the World, Including the East Indies: The Rise and Progress of the Funding System Explained*, by Patrick Colquhoun in London, 1814.

Highest Order: Royal family, Lords and Great Officers of State, all above the degree or rank of a Baronet, with their families.

Some peerage ranks in order of importance: duke, marquess, earl, viscount, baron. The highest rank of the peerage, duke, is the most exclusive.

Second Class: Baronets, knights, country gentleman and others with a vast fortune and income along with their families. Baronets are a step below a baron. They have never sat in the House of Lords and they're the hereditary equivalent of a knighthood. Baronets are made up of commoners, designated by "Sir" before the name and Baronet, (usually abbreviated *Bart.)*, for example: *Sir John Smith, Bart.*

Third Class: Clergy, prestigious positions in the State (government jobs), elevated senior positions in law and medicine, successful merchants and manufacturers, bankers and their families.

Fourth Class: These people hold lesser positions in the Church as well as in government. Occupations include: Those who practice law or medicine, teachers, ship owners, land owners (real estate), and lesser merchants and smaller manufacturers. It also includes artists, respectable shopkeepers, respectable builders, mechanics, and those with moderate incomes and their families.

Fifth Class: Lesser shopkeepers, Inn keepers, those in public service (civil servant), miscellaneous occupations, and others living on moderate income with their families.

Sixth Class: Working mechanics, lesser artisans, those who produce handicrafts, agricultural labor, menial servants, and other manual labor and their families.

Seventh Class (Lower Class): Vagrants, gypsy, vagabonds, and disorderly persons who are supported by criminal delinquency.

Army and Navy: Commissioned and non-commissioned officers of the Army, Navy, Marines, as well as all Soldiers, and Seamen, including all officers on half-pay, retired, and pensioners and their families.

21st Century Class Structure: 2001 UK Office of National Statistics (ONS)

Group	Description
1	Higher professional and managerial occupations
2	Lower managerial and professional occupations
3	Intermediate occupations
4	Small employers and own account workers
5	Lower supervisory and technical occupations
6	Semi-routine occupations
7	Routine occupations
8	Never worked and long-term unemployed

The National Statistics Socio-economic Classification (often abbreviated to NS-SEC) is the official socio-economic classification in the United Kingdom. It is an adaptation of the Goldthorpe schema which was first known as the Nuffield Class Schema developed in the 1970s

21st Century Class Structure: 2017 Great British Class Survey:

Taken from University of Manchester April 2, 2017, analysis of the results of the Great British Class Survey (GBCS; a survey of social class in the United Kingdom).

Elite: Top six (6) percent of British society. Occupations such as chief executive officers, IT and telecommunications directors, marketing and sales directors; functional managers and directors, judges, lawyers (barristers and solicitors), accountants, financial managers, doctors, dentists, professors and advertising and public relations directors. Households in 2011 earned £89,000; average house price was £325,000.

Elites may also include trust-fund recipients and children of very wealthy families. These are adults who have inherited an allowance and possibly housing, so they do not need to hold a job. Some may be employed because they want to be, but an income for them is not necessary "to pay the bills".

<u>Established middle class:</u> About 25 percent of British society. Occupations included: electrical engineers, occupational therapists, midwives, environmental professionals, police constables, quality assurance and regulatory professionals, town-planning officials, and special-needs teaching professionals. Household income averaged £47,000 a year. Home value averaged £177,000. They had an average savings of £26,000.

<u>Technical middle class:</u> About six (6) percent of British society. Occupations: medical radiographers, aircraft pilots, pharmacists, natural and social science professionals as well as physical scientists, senior professionals in education establishments, and business, research, and administrative positions. Household incomes averaged £38,000, average savings of £66,000 and houses worth an average of £163,000.

<u>New affluent workers</u> About 15 percent of British society. Occupations include: electricians and electrical fitters; postal workers; retail cashiers and checkout operatives; plumbers and heating and ventilation engineers; sales and retail assistants; housing officers; kitchen and catering assistants; quality assurance technicians. Many are young people in white collar and blue collar jobs in the private sector and in customer facing occupations. Household income is moderate; average savings is small with average house value was £129,000 as of 2011.

Traditional working class: About 14 percent of British society. Occupations include: electrical and electronics technicians; care workers; cleaners; van drivers; electricians; residential, day, and domiciliary care. Few are graduates, many filling traditional working-class occupations such as lorry (truck) drivers, cleaners, electrician and menial white collar occupations and any of the professions listed in the Emergent sector but they do have secure housing and income. Many are women. Household income of only £13,000. However, many own their homes, with an average value in 2011 of £127,000.

Emergent service sector About 19 percent of British society. Occupations include bar staff, bartenders, wait-staff in restaurants, chefs, nursing auxiliaries and assistants, assemblers and routine operatives, care workers, elementary storage occupations, customer service occupations, musicians. They may only get paid when they perform or work, so may have insecure housing and irregular income stream. Emergent service sector workers are relatively young with an average age of 34. Typical occupations are bar work, chef, customer service and call centre workers. They fill a wide variety of low-paid service sector slots. Average household income of £21,000.

Precariat:

This group is formed by people suffering from **"precarity"**, which is an unstable economic condition. Their work income is not predictable nor secure, causing them stress.

About 15 percent of British society. Occupations include cleaners, van drivers, care workers (elder care workers and child care workers and grounds keepers), carpenters, and some retail cashiers, joiners, caretakers, leisure and travel service occupations, shopkeepers and proprietors, and retail cashiers. Average household income of £8,000, negligible savings, who usually rent. Characterized by high amounts of income insecurity.

End of Conversation Station for this Volume 11

12ᵗʰ Volume Confrontation

Volume's Theme

Confrontation

Isaiah 27:4 (New International Version NIV) ...If only there were briers and thorns confronting me! I would march against them in battle; I would set them all on fire.

Chapters Referenced

Preparation for Group

RESORTS conduct conversations with: *Respect, Empathy, Sources, Opportunity, Rebuttal, Timing, Speculation. See page 12.*

Group Leader Will Need:

✧ List of helpful inventions from the 1700's

This is a proposed cadence for conducting a structured session where the group host or instructor will keep the group members on track and usher the members from one section to the next with a specific output obtained by the end of the session.

Structured Activity 1

In Firebrand we see resourceful characters who helped others. List inventions which were created during the 1700's to help others. Which is your favorite invention?

Structured Activity 2

List countries which had immigrants in the Colonies during the 1700's. Which local tribes made alliances with which country? Which languages were spoken?

Structured Activity 3

How do you pool resources to develop a new invention? If the other party you work with confronts you, how do overcome that barrier in order to collaborate? Would you handle that challenge differently in the 1700's as opposed to today? Document similarities and differences between how you would handle confrontation and develop peaceful relations in the 18th century versus today.

<u>Objective Achieved:</u> Understand what motivated developing inventions and how collaborations and alliances formed in the 1700s as different cultures and languages blended.

<u>Group Conversation</u>

This is the proposed method of guiding a group in an open ended discussion. It could be different each time as the discussion may take various directions. The group host's responsibility is to remind the group when the time is coming to a close, and thank them for the group participation.

.

This is a set of questions. The trajectory of the conversation can take you in almost any direction. As the moderator or group leader and instructor, be prepared to remind the group that discussion should be respectful, fact-based, or if based on the speaker's opinion, is stated as such in advance, before sharing their ideas in this public forum.

In this forum, you can analyze character motivations and speculate about what might happen to the character even beyond the storyline in these Firebrand volumes. To ensure that no one speaker monopolizes the conversation, you may want to limit each comment to a specified duration of time, such as three to five minutes, and then allow other group members to respond.

1) Have you ever had to directly face a fear and do everything you could to get out of that situation? How did you handle that?

2) Do you agree with how Jane reacted to situations versus how Mr. Tweedbottom reacted? If you were in either Jane's position or Mr. Tweedbottom's position, would you have reacted differently? How would your reaction have affected the outcome of the story?

3) Have you had a relationship where you trusted somebody but then discovered their motives were not pure or that they intended to harm or betray you? How did you deal with that?

4) Eliza reached out to try and help, but she could not. Have you ever figuratively tried to help but found your efforts were not enough for the situation? What did you do? How did you handle it? What would you do next time?

5) What did you think of the way Susanna behaved as

she hurried about her business. Did she do anything to surprise you? What were her motives? What does Billy think of her?

6) Even if you disagree with somebody, how do you show them that you have viewed the situation from their point of view before forming your opinion? How do you convey that you understand another viewpoint?

To close the group discussion, thank the group for their participation and offer them the option to do an activity after the group is dismissed.

Remind the group to know when to confront and when to wait. Discernment is valuable and essential.

Assignments (Optional)

Optional assignments are suggested here for your participants to work on after the group discussion has ended. Encourage enthusiasm and proper research procedures. Invite your group to share their findings with each other at the next session, or you can have them submit their work directly to you, the group leader.

Make a list of how you could better understand the perspective of another person:

1) How does the other person process new information? Do they need to see pictures, hear a story, write down notes, converse informally, memorize short facts?

2) How do you process information, and how can you share a new idea with somebody who process it differently?

3) When looking at a new issue, do you ask who, what , when, where, and why BEFORE you come to a conclusion?

End of Conversation Station for this Volume 12

13th Volume Deliverance

Volume's Theme

Deliverance

Psalm 82:4 (21st Century King James) Deliver the poor and needy; rescue them out of the hand of the wicked.

Psalm 144:11 (21st century King James) Rescue me and deliver me from the hand of strangers, whose mouth speaketh vanity and whose right hand is a right hand of falsehood,

Chapters Referenced

1 CHAPTER 129: (JULY 4, 1776) Room For One More
2 CHAPTER 130: (JULY 4, 1776) Bryce At Sea
3 CHAPTER 131: (JULY 4, 1776-6:00am) Feather
4 CHAPTER 132: (JULY 4, 1776 3:00AM) FLASHBACK Churning Waters-Hours earlier
5 CHAPTER 133: (JULY 4, 1776-3:05am) Bryce Splashed
6 CHAPTER 134: (JULY 4, 1776 3:10AM to 5:00AM) – Bryce Bobbing In Water
7 CHAPTER 135: (JULY 4, 1776 –7:00AM) The Boat Returns
8 CHAPTER 136: (JULY 4, 1776) Following Susanna to Philadelphia, Pennsylvania
9 CHAPTER 137: (JULY 4, 1776) The Balcony
10 CHAPTER 138: (JULY 4, 1776) Mrs. Dunlap and the Scroll
11 CHAPTER 139: (JULY 4, 1776) Waiting Outside
12 CHAPTER 140: (JULY 4, 1776) Unexpected Arrival

Preparation for Group

RESORTS conduct conversations with: *Respect, Empathy, Sources, Opportunity, Rebuttal, Timing, Speculation. See page 12.*

Group Leader Will Need:

✧ List of Colonial heroes, professions, and actions which can be done today. Be able to share some hero names if the group cannot think of any.

This is a proposed cadence for conducting a structured session where the group host or instructor will keep the group members on track and usher the members from one section to the next with a specific output obtained by the end of the session.

Structured Activity 1

Which characters in Firebrand do you think act heroically? What real-life Colonial people (male and female) do you think acted heroically? Why do you think their actions were heroic?

Structured Activity 2

List professions of the 1770's in the Colonies which would have been made difficult given British occupation. For example, running a printing press. Were these professions heroic? Why?

Structured Activity 3

List ways you can be a hero to somebody else in modern times.

How would you go about making a difference to one person or to a group of people?

What would be your heroic motto to remind you why you do what you are doing?

Objective Achieved: Participants are able to state how to give back to community with achievable heroic acts.

Group Conversation

This is the proposed method of guiding a group in an open ended discussion. It could be different each time as the discussion may take various directions. The group host's responsibility is to remind the group when the time is coming to a close, and thank them for the group participation.

.

This is a set of questions. The trajectory of the conversation can take you in almost any direction. As the moderator or group leader and instructor, be prepared to remind the group that discussion should be respectful, fact-based, or if based on the speaker's opinion, is stated as such in advance, before sharing their ideas in this public forum.

In this forum, you can analyze character motivations and speculate about what might happen to the character even beyond the storyline in these Firebrand volumes. To ensure that no one speaker monopolizes the conversation, you may want to limit each comment to a specified duration of time, such as three to five minutes, and then allow other group members to respond.

1) When in a bad situation do you look to others to rescue you or do you try and figure a way out yourself? Why?

2) Have you ever felt that one event could solve all your problems, such as "win the jackpot" or "get a new X to make everything better" when confronting bad situations? Have you ever tried to make small changes to yourself to avoid repeating bad situations?

3) How would you behave if you realized that nobody was going to come and rescue you? What would you do differently? How do you demonstrate that you are taking responsibility for the good and bad? How do you respond with integrity and honor to avoid being pulled down into a petty argument and instead, focus on solving the problem?

103

4) When trying to solve a problem all by yourself, at what point do you reach out to somebody else?

5) Envision the typical melodrama: A damsel in distress held captive by an evil villain waiting for the hero to rescue her.

Do you view yourself as the villain who *inflicts* problems, or the *victim* who is always entangled with problems, or are you the *rescuer* who recognizes victims and saves them?

Why do you think you are that way and should you change or stay the same?

6) What did you think of the rescue described in this volume? What did you like and not like about it?

7) Do you think "luck" happens or is it really an opportunity you notice at the time you are working hard on making the situation better? Do you think the characters in *Firebrand* were "lucky", or did their integrity help them make the correct small choices to lead them to cross paths with each other and make an even bigger impact by combining forces?

To close the group discussion, thank the group for their participation and offer them the option to do an activity after the group is dismissed. Sometimes they will need to be rescued and sometimes they will need to rescue others. Appreciate the perspective of the other side.

Assignments (Optional)

Optional assignments are suggested here for your participants to work on after the group discussion has ended. Encourage enthusiasm and proper research procedures. Invite your group to share their findings with each other at the next session, or you can have them submit their work directly to you, the group leader.

1. List problems which you may face in the future.

2. List actions you can take to make the situation better.

3. List what preparations are needed to execute that action seamlessly.

4. What skills are needed to practice in order to improve? Set a date when you will start doing a bit of that practice each day or week or month so that you are prepared for when that situation may arise. You'll be able to better handle it.

End of Conversation Station for this Volume 13

14ᵗʰ Volume Wisdom

Volume's Theme

Wisdom

Proverbs 9:9 (Common English Bible) Teach the wise, and they will become wiser; inform the righteous, and their learning will increase.

Proverbs 3:13 (New International Version NIV) Blessed are those who find wisdom, those who gain understanding.

Chapters Referenced

1 CHAPTER 141: (JULY 4, 1776) Come Inside the Church, Says the Magistrate
2 CHAPTER 142: (JULY 3, 1776) Hours Earlier aboard the SPY
3 CHAPTER 143: (JULY 3, 1776): Jane Dangles
4 CHAPTER 144: (JULY 3, 1776) Just After That...
5 CHAPTER 145: (JULY 4, 1776) The Search Continues for Bryce, Early Morning
6 CHAPTER 146: (JULY 4, 1776) Pew Pondering. How did You Survive?
7 CHAPTER 147: (JULY 4, 1776) Jane Wanted to See the Document Signed
8 CHAPTER 148: (JULY 4, 1776) The Second Proposal
9 CHAPTER 149: (JULY 4, 1776) The Meeting Adjourns
10 CHAPTER 150: (JULY 4, 1776) Getting the Carriage...

Preparation for Group

RESORTS conduct conversations with: *Respect, Empathy, Sources, Opportunity, Rebuttal, Timing, Speculation. See page 12.*

Group Leader Will Need:

- ✧ Picture of a sailing vessel from the 1770's

- ✧ Place to write lists

This is a proposed cadence for conducting a structured session where the group host or instructor will keep the group members on track and usher the members from one section to the next with a specific output obtained by the end of the session.

Structured Activity 1

Write how life may have been on the ship from Europe to American and back to Europe.

Structured Activity 2

Write what is needed to start life in the colonies. How would you get to know new friends or make business contacts?

Write out a time-line of when important documents were signed, which influenced the formation of the United states.

Structured Activity 3

What things would you have been used to in Europe but were not available in the Colonies? What substitutes would you use? For example, if tea was scarce in the Colonies, would you drink coffee? If whalebone under-garments were scarce, what other material would you use?

Objective Achieved: Describe the thought process Colonists had to go thorough to make wise choices in the 18ᵗʰ century.

Group Conversation

This is the proposed method of guiding a group in an open ended discussion. It could be different each time as the discussion may take various directions. The group host's responsibility is to remind the group when the time is coming to a close, and thank them for the group participation.

.

This is a set of questions. The trajectory of the conversation can take you in almost any direction. As the moderator or group leader and instructor, be prepared to remind the group that discussion should be respectful, fact-based, or if based on the speaker's opinion, is stated as such in advance, before sharing their ideas in this public forum.

In this forum, you can analyze character motivations and speculate about what might happen to the character even beyond the storyline in these Firebrand volumes. To ensure that no one speaker monopolizes the conversation, you may want to limit each comment to a specified duration of time, such as three to five minutes, and then allow other group members to respond.

1) What process do you go through before deciding what is the right action to take?

2) How do you give advice to others? Do people ask you for your advice, or do you offer it before they ask? What reactions to you get from people when they hear your advice?

3) What is your opinion of the ship SPY?

4) What is your opinion regarding Silversmith's invention? What else could be considered insignificant until a dire situation arises and then that innovation becomes very useful?

A long time ago, did you create something, and then recently found a useful purpose for your innovation?

5) State your opinion of the significance regarding what occurred in the meeting?

6) Which current events do you think may have a lasting impact on the future? Would that impact last 100 years from today? Would that be a good or bad effect?

To close the group discussion, thank the members for their participation and offer them the option to do an activity after the group is dismissed.

Remind the group that there is always more to the story than what they see on the surface. Advise and encourage them to make all their choices in life wisely, as the consequences may last for years into the future.

Assignments (Optional)

Optional assignments are suggested here for your participants to work on after the group discussion has ended. Encourage enthusiasm and proper research procedures. Invite your group to share their findings with each other at the next session, or you can have them submit their work directly to you, the group leader.

Conduct some research and hunt down how many peace treaties were crafted during the 1700's. Did these peace treaties allow for local economic prosperity for the parties who signed? Was it wise, in your opinion, to have drafted, negotiated, and agreed to these peace treaties?

End of Conversation Station for this Volume 14

15ᵗʰ Volume Holidays

Note: *Since this is the final volume of* **Firebrand**, *you have more choices for your optional activity. You can have a Colonial themed party! You can save the conversation questions for the party. You can dress up in 18ᵗʰ century fashions. You can host an art contest. You can find dancing styles and popular songs from the Colonial period and try them out! You can locate recipes and cook dishes from that period for everyone in your group to sample. Or you can have a Colonial bake-off contest. Be creative. You have a jubilant variety of celebration options! Have a wonderful time!*

Volume's Theme

Holidays

Esther 2:18 (New Living Translation   NLT To celebrate the occasion,   he gave a great banquet ... declaring a public holiday ...

Chapters Referenced

Preparation for Group

RESORTS conduct conversations with: *Respect, Empathy, Sources, Opportunity, Rebuttal, Timing, Speculation. See page 12.*

Group Leader Will Need:

✧ A blank map of the colonies to be filled in during group session.

✧ Picture of the Liberty bell.

This is a proposed cadence for conducting a structured session where the group host or instructor will keep the group members on track and usher the members from one section to the next with a specific output obtained by the end of the session.

Structured Activity I

Take the colonies and plot them on a map. List the date when they became an official Colony.

1) Connecticut
2) Delaware
3) Georgia
4) Maryland
5) Massachusetts
6) New
Hampshire
7) New Jersey
8) New York
9) North Carolina
10) Rhode Island
11) Pennsylvania
12) South
Carolina
13) Virginia

Structured Activity 2

Imagine you need to start your own colony. Write a list:

1) What do you need to organize a group of people if they are going to be residents in your colony?

2) Given the existing 13 colonies, which location would you select? Claim it on a map.

3) What is the weather there and what sort of seasons do you need to prepare for?

4) Can you review an almanac for other colonies in that area during that time to extrapolate what sort of weather issues you may need to face? How would you prepare your residents for this weather challenge?

5) What crops grow in that area? What would be a "product" you and your colony would create, share, and barter with other Colonists? Would you export this product to Europe?

6) What economic activities would you conduct on a regular basis? How would you train the children in your colony to learn a profession?

7) If you created a product to be exported, how would you get your product to port so it could be shipped and withstand a long voyage to Europe?

8) How many people will your colony need to support?

How quickly will it grow each year?

9) List two Pros and two Cons about this colony?

10) How will your colony be governed? Will you try to meet and align with the other colonial governors?

11) Who creates the laws and how are those laws enforced? What would be the first three laws you want to establish for the residents of your colony? How would you keep your residents safe from foreign attacks, wildlife, weather elements, or other nearby colonies who may just want your territory for themselves?

12) What sorts of livestock will your colonists keep and what will you feed those animals? What would be common reasons this type of livestock may need medical (veterinarian) services? How would those services be regulated in your colony?

13) What tools do you need to build a home in 1776?

14) How would you embark on crafting a peace treaty? With which parties do you need to establish peace?

15) How would you create tools? For example, do you need to set up a blacksmith shop? How would you do that?

16) How would you create clothing?

17) How would you record, document, and enforce territory boundaries of your residents? How would you create a map? How would you handle boundary

disputes between residents? How would you enforce the outer boundary of the entire colony?

18) How would you keep your colony sanitary? How would you manage waste generated by residents? How would you secure food and clean water?

19) How might a visiting guest obtain food, water, and lodging?

Structured Activity 3

Write a short fictional story about how you think the liberty bell got cracked and why it did not get fixed.

You can write a story by yourself, or as a group.

Note which elements are fictional and which are based on genuine fact.

Share the story with the group.

Objective Achieved: Be able to explain the process of governing a colony or colonies, in general.

Group Conversation

This is the proposed method of guiding a group in an open ended discussion. It could be different each time as the discussion may take various directions. The group host's responsibility is to remind the group when the time is coming to a close, and thank them for the group participation.

.

This is a set of questions. The trajectory of the conversation can take you in almost any direction. As the moderator or group leader and instructor, be prepared to remind the group that discussion should be respectful, fact-based, or if based on the speaker's opinion, is stated as such in advance, before sharing their ideas in this public forum.

In this forum, you can analyze character motivations and speculate about what might happen to the character even beyond the storyline in these Firebrand volumes. To ensure that no one speaker monopolizes the conversation, you may want to limit each comment to a specified duration of time, such as three to five minutes, and then allow other group members to respond.

1) How do you celebrate holidays?

2) What events do you celebrate which are not formal holidays? How do you celebrate them?

3) Share what do you think about the American holiday Independence day? What personal memories are triggered when you think of this day?

4) Explain your perspective regarding the wedding in this story?

5) If Silversmith was taught the skill to read and write, tell what you think about her desire to write a book, which could be passed from one generation to the next.

6) What did you think about the way the story *Firebrand* ended? Do you agree with the fate of all the characters? What do you think will happen next in the unwritten story which occurs later after this tale?

7) State your opinion about making small choices, either good or bad, and how those decisions could impact future generations?

8) GROUP LEADER: Read this aloud to the group and ask for feedback about it:

  a) *To gather the names of all those representing the colonies took some time. There were also copies made of the Declaration of Independence, but the version with all the signatures was labeled on the back as the original.*

  b) *The German version was printed and distributed to all the German speaking people living in the colonies. It was later translated into French and published in Philadelphia in 1778.*

c) *In the Declaration of Independence, Thomas Jefferson wanted to condemn the British for promoting the slave trade, but this was removed in the version which was signed.*

d) *As soon as the Declaration of Independence was read out loud to the troops governed by George Washington and other colonists, they rushed into Bowling Green Park in Lower Manhattan and tore down the 4,000 pound gold-covered lead statue of King George the third on horseback. Another gentleman who signed the document, General Oliver Wolcott, had the scrap metal brought back to his home in Litchfield, Connecticut, to be melted down into 40,000 bullets, which were all used in the Revolutionary War.*

9) GROUP LEADER: Discuss these possible continuing story lines, which are not in *Firebrand*. The group can speculate and use their imagination to answer the next set of questions. Since this set of group questions require imagination, there are no right nor wrong answers:

a) Eliza Lucas may make a sky blue silk cloth for Jane to have a dress made. This would be a late wedding present for Jane. Because it could take a year to craft a dress, do you think this is why there is a modern day tradition to give gifts to wedded couples up to one year after the wedding took place?

b) Why do you think Susanna wanted to give a swatch of blue silk to Benjamin Franklin? In promoting American-made (United-Colony-made) products, do you think he could have impressed a royal princesses by showing off the high quality product which united colonies could export?

c) Do you think that Eliza Lucas and Magistrate Pinkney formally courted and married? Do you think his heart was "true blue" for Eliza? Do you think he was proud of her business expertise since she developed a formula for American Indigo blue, which could have been used as a stable substitute for currency during a time with the economy was unsettled? In real life, who did Eliza really marry and who did the Magistrate of the town really marry? How might life be different today if different people married each other in 1770?

d) Do you think that Billy Dawes, the driver, got a job working for Bryce Aiden Tyler and Jane? Do you think that Bryce used his business savvy to set Billy up in his own business? Do you think Billy and Silversmith got married? Do you think that Silversmith and Billy collaborated to improve the delivery of mail, newspapers and parcels and improve roads so carriages could more easily travel?

e) Do you think Susanna Wright did connect with

the Swedish sailor who had helped Button? Did the Swedish sailor and Susanna get married? Do you think Susanna's love of American silks and the Sailor's knowledge of merchant routes would help them create a niche business becoming wealthy? Do you think Susanna did weave the sky blue Indigo dyed silk and oversaw the making of a dress in time for Jane's first wedding anniversary to ring in the new year of 1777?

f) Do you think that the man of the cloth, who Christened Polly and Button's child as Bjorn Esterday on July 4th, 1776 eventually developed a romance or got married to Polly's mother?

g) What do you think of a tradition such as naming the first born son Bjorn for every generation in your family from the 1770's onward? What sense of history would that give to the person bearing that name? Do you think they would feel obligated to act with honor, wisdom, and integrity? Do you think the name Bjorn Esterday symbolizes independence, freedom, family, hope and love?

To close the group discussion, thank the group for their participation and offer them the option to do an activity after the group is dismissed.

Since this is the final volume of the *Firebrand* series, do inform the group participants that they should celebrate as if it were a holiday, just as the characters in the book celebrated.

Assignments (Optional)

Optional assignments are suggested here for your participants to work on after the group discussion has ended. Encourage enthusiasm and proper research procedures. Invite your group to share their findings with each other, or you can have them submit their work directly to you, the group leader.

This is the final episode, so the assignment is to organize a Colonial themed celebration for all participants.

End of Conversation Station for the entire *Firebrand* Series. We had a wonderful time and hope your created grand lasting memories!

16 Vocabulary (Alphabetized)

Many archaic terms are used commonly in the 1770s, but might be considered unfamiliar if used today. This section lists a compilation of the vocabulary terms located at the back of each of the *Firebrand* volumes. There may be terms or words used in the volumes which is not defined in this list. Group participants are encouraged to investigate a modern or etymological (historical origins) dictionary to fully understand the term beyond what is defined herein.

Absurd: Foolish, silly.

Accessible: Easy to reach.

Acquaintance: A person known to you, but not a close friend.

Akan: This is a term referencing the residents

of modern day West Africa, which includes Ghana. This term has been in use since around the 1690's.

Alight / Alighted: To step down from Allgemeine Literatur-Zeitung is a newspaper which started around 1785 by Friedrich Justin Bertuch, "the father of the German periodical."

Almanac: A reference book with calendars, lists, charts, etc.

Attribute: A quality or description of someone or something.

Bight of Biafra: "Byht" is a term from Old English which indicates the meaning "bend, angle, corner." In this story, it references an area of land which may be shaped to be pliable and curved, narrow and long, a portion of the coastline in modern day West Africa. This has been in use since the 15th century. Old maps from the 1500's to 1700's indicate this region with the terms Biafra, Biafara,and Biafares. This could reference the modern day Cameroon, by the Niger River. It may be referenced as Golfe du Biafra locally. The

West African "Republic of Biafra", existed from May 1967 to January 1970.

Blancs: This refers to face make up used which gave the face a white color. Some say this is reminiscent of the Japanese Geisha make up. Some say it was the precursor to modern-day foundation, which today is the color of your skin. This early fashion trend was popular in Venice, Italy. It referred to blanc de ceruse de Venise or Spirits of Saturn. A recipe from 1688, "Magistry of Saturn and Lead", shows the lead face-paint was a mixture of water, vinegar and lead. The lead caused hair loss as it was absorbed through the skin and by inhalation. Cheaper, less expensive, Ceruse would substitute chalk for the more popular lead.

Bumroll: This is a padding which was considered fashionable for women to wear to achieve a specific silhouette with their skirts. Bumroll or Rump-pad- This was an undergarment usually stuffed with cork or other firm yet light-weight stuffing inside a linen or cotton case and tied around the waist. This would be over the pannier and petticoat, but under the outer skirt. Sometimes ladies would wear this instead of a pannier, but several wore it on top of a pannier.

Chemise: This is sometimes called a "shift" and modern terms would be "slip". This was a sheath of fabric made of cotton or linen or silk. It was the garment which touched the skin and served as the foundation for all the other garments layered on top. It extended from the knees to the calf area of your leg.   Both men and women wore a shift. A woman must never be seen in just a chemise as she would be considered "un-clothed". Only her ladies maid or her husband could see her in such a state.

Coffers: A strong box for saving money or valuables, such as jewelry.

Colophon: An emblem or statement used by printers to indicate who authored the work and other printing details. Typically it could be found on the spine, end, or cover of most printed works.

Compliant: Ready to agree. Yielding.

Condemneth: This is an old fashioned way of saying you blame or condemn a person. It is as if it were saying "he who blames the good" or "He who blames or frames an innocent person for a crime they never committed...."

Consternation: Extreme surprise with confusion and fear.

Count Ewald Friedrich von Hertzberg: Born 1725- 1795 (age 69) became a lawyer in 1745 and became a director in the Prussian state archives by 1750.

This started his career to influence international politics with the goal of preserving the interests of Prussia.

In 1752 he married Baroness Marie von Knyphausen. Earlier he was hailed by his king for making peace with Sweden (1757). He also negotiated peace with the Treaty of Hubertsburg (1763) and was congratulated by the king with,"I congratulate you. You have made peace as I made war, one against many."

He also took part successfully as a publicist in the negotiations concerning the question of the Bavarian succession (1778) and those of the peace of Teschen (1779).

Much later he penned a letter to George Washington (14 June 1793).

Dactylopius coccus: Today we may reference this bug as the cochineal. It had been used to give the British military coats it's red color. Some say that these bugs will cluster on Opuntia cactus pads. There had been discussions in the colonies that if ever they were going to form a militia, they would not use the red color as the British had done, they would need to find another substance specific to their land. Indeed, they may have settled on the deep blue of Indigo, which is from a plant. Starting on page 71, Eliza explains how she makes Indigo dye.

Daughters Of Liberty: These were the women who wove fabric to make clothing for their families so that they could boycott the purchase of British fabrics. This started around the year 1765.

Debris: Something torn or broken which is scattered around.

Decline: To say "no". To refuse. Or to bend, or slant.

Define: To describe the meaning of a word, or what an object does or looks like.

Discourage: To oppose. To give up hope.

Distraught: Upset and worried.

Divide et impera: This means "divide and conquer". This is a political strategy to cause conflict within your opponent's group in order to weaken them.
If you successfully divide the strength of your opponent when they are fighting among themselves, then it will be much easier to conquer them...

Divo/ Primo Uomo: *Divo* is Italian for a prominent tenor. The form of the word assigned to a female is "*Diva*". Another term used to indicate a starring male singer is "*Primo Uomo*". The female version is "*Prima Donna*"....

Doeskin britch and moccasins: This references the leather from a doe (mature female deer) made into pants which covered a man from his waist to his knees. The moccasins were shoes worn on the feet. The term "Britch" was used in the 1620's, but by 1905 the term "Britches" was used.

Drawing room: A room in a house where visitors may be entertained.

Emit / Emitted: Give out a sound, or give out liquid, or heat, or light.

Encounter: To meet.
ensnare, betray and profit- These were terms used to summarize the methods of slave traders.

Ensnare: is to capture. Betray is to gain the trust of another and then prove yourself untrustworthy, false and ready to violate all trust between two parties. "Profit", in the "slave trade", means to gain money by selling another human into a captive situation they do not want, but you force anyway because you will make money.

Epiphany: A moment when you suddenly feel that you understand. (The first recognition of the true nature of Christ by the gentiles.)

Estate: A big piece of land with gardens and a grand fancy house.

Etching: The art of making designs on metal, glass, etc. by using acid. The picture or figure made this way is also called an etching.

Fashionable: Wearing clothes, doing things, going places that are popular at a particular time.

Feign: To pretend, or to act in a way you do not feel

Fop or Foppish: "Fop" is a term for a man who is so obsessed with how he looks and the clothing he is wearing and how to behave that it overshadows everything else. It is not a flattering term.

Foppish Originally used around the 1600's, this term described a man who is foolishly obsessed with how he appears, concerned more with shoe-buckles and lace-cuffs and taking a substance to make him feel elated, focusing only on his own comforts rather than upon matters which would impact those around him.

Fortnight: this is a two-week period of time. This was a term used in the 17th century (1600's). The Old English is *feowertyne niht*, which means "fourteen nights". Today you may hear the term "biweekly" or "every two weeks"....

Foyer: Just inside the main door, the foyer is a room which leads to the rest of the house.

Gauche: To lack social grace. To be crude, clumsy, awkward.

Greatcoat: This is an archaic term originating from around the 1660's. It references an overcoat or a heavy coat to wear over all your other clothing.

Headrights: This was a term used in the 17th and 18th centuries to grant a pioneer a parcel of land. Frequently this was about 50 acres of land to encourage settlement in untamed regions.

Hypnotic / hypnotize: Keeps your attention. With hypnotic suggestion, a person can be made sleepy and then follows directions.

Ingratiate: To gain the favor of someone by being very nice.

Inspired: Brilliant, outstanding, as if done by divine direction.

Interject: To throw other things in between. To interrupt or talk while another person is still speaking.

Jacquard: A type of fabric which contains a woven pattern within the fabric. These were woven by hand, so became a symbol of wealth and status. One day, a weaver, Joseph Marie Jacquard, created a more efficient device which required less labor and still could create woven designs in the fabric. He created the "jacquard" with his Jacquard Mechanism system or loom.

Jest: A joke. Talking with good-natured fun. To speak in a playful way.

Jetsamed: Pushing away. The Jetsam is a part of a ship, or the cargo on the ship or any equipment used to operate the ship which is heaved overboard to lighten the load during a time when the ship is in trouble and must shed weight so it can remain afloat. Often, that which was heaved overboard either sinks or is washed ashore. In the 1560's the word "Jottsome" was an act of throwing goods overboard to lighten a ship. The old French word is "getaison ". A modern version of the word is "Jettison". In the 1590's the word "Flotsam" was used as "goods thrown away overboard" "Flotsam and Jetsam"

Justifieth: This is an old fashioned way of saying "he who makes an excuse for bad behavior..."

Licensing: The government gives a person or group special permission to do something.

Lorgnette: This was a tool to improve one's vision. Some would bring these to theaters so that they could get a close view of the performers on the stage. It is similar to modern-day binoculars except Lorgnettes were often embellished to be a fashion accessory with formal evening attire. Additionally, one end was often on a stick-like stand so the user could hold it while resting an elbow on the ledge of an opera box to gaze upon the actors on the stage below.

Luminescence: Light shining at a low temperature because of chemical changes. Luminescence (or "cold light") is any emission of light (electromagnetic waves) from a substance that does not arise from heating.

This definition makes luminescence distinct from **incandescence** which is light emission due to the elevated temperature of a substance, such as a glowing hot ember. Luminescence may be seen in neon and fluorescent lamps, lightning and the aurora borealis.

Photoluminescence is the process of a substance emitting light after that material has absorbed light. The absorption of electromagnetic radiation is done by a substance called a phosphor. Light emission is triggered by the absorption of photons. **Florescence** is quick photoluminescence. **Phosphorescence** is long-lived photoluminescence that continues long after the photoexcitation has stopped.

In other words, if the substance was exposed to radiation and that radiation was removed, the substance which has phosphorescence will have an afterglow, which could last a long time, longer than fluorescence, depending on the situation.

To simplify it, *Incandescence* occurs when a substance is heated until it glows. *Luminescence* occurs when a substance glows for any reason besides heat.

If that glow is caused by photons hitting atoms, that type of luminescence is called *photoluminescence.*

If the glow is caused by electrons, then that type of luminescence is called *electroluminescence.* If the glow is caused by a chemical reaction, that sort of glow is called *chemiluminescence.*

If the glow occurs when the type of chemical reaction occurs in vivo, then that type of luminescence is called *bioluminescence.*

By the way, *in vivo* means it happens inside a living organism or natural setting. *In vitro* means it happens inside a laboratory vessel or a controlled environment.

If the glow (luminescence) lasts a long time (from 10 nanoseconds to years), after the source causing the glow has been removed, then it is called *phosphorescence.* If, however, the glow only lasts for 10 nanoseconds or less, then it is called *fluorescence.*

Malfeasance is a word meaning an official misconduct, a violation of a public trust or obligation. A term used since the 1690s.

Malfeasant is a person or "wrong-doer" who has done an act which is positively unlawful or wrongful. It is a person who transgresses moral or civil law. The French word *malfaisance* is translated to mean "wrongdoing".

Mandated: A formal order from a higher official to act or speak in a certain way.

Marchioness: Marchioness de Waldegrave was one name used by Sarah Wilson. This is a royal title. "Marchioness" is in the ranks of royal peerage: Other royal titles are:
    For men, King and for ladies Queen;
    For men, Prince and for ladies Princess;
    For men, Duke and for ladies, Duchess;
    For men, Marquess and for ladies, Marchioness;
    For men, Earl and for ladies Countess;
    For men, Viscount and for ladies Viscountess;
    For men, Baron and for ladies Baroness.

Middling: Before the concepts of "Upper class", "Middle class", and "Lower class", people recognized status by their titles. This separated government workers from royals, or even farmers. People who held a trade were called "middling people" and may have been the start of the working class - or middle class, meaning they had to learn a skill so they could hold a job to earn money to pay the bills.
They did not have an allowance or "trust fund" to pay their bills.

Milano: This is the name of the city of Milan in Italy.

Non-verbal: Not using written or spoken words. Using gestures and facial expressions, instead.

Nya Sveriga: The was a Swedish term for "New Sweden", one of the original New World areas settled.

Obnoxious: Badly behaved, rude, offensive.

Orikata or Papiroflexia: This was a term used for paper folding. Today we may reference this art of paper-folding as "origami".

Overskirts: When ladies would dress, they had underskirts, or skirts which whey wore underneath their outer skirts They also had overskirts, which were usually below-ankle-length skirts which would be visible and conceal the undergarments.

Pannier: Some may call this undergarment a "hoop skirt". Pannier comes from the French word for "basket" and resembled a bird cage shape.

This was a garment which was used underneath the outer skirt to provide volume. Around the 1720's large dome-shaped skirts were considered fashionable.

The larger your "hips" meant you could afford more fabric of the skirt to cover it, which implied you had sufficient wealth to spend on extra fabric. By the 1730's the pannier became a rounded oval shape. By 1745, it became wide, oblong at the hips, and flat on the front and rear of the skirt. Around 1770, a rounded hoop-skirt was coming into fashion.

The underskirt, or Pannier, held its shape by using a frame of wood, whalebone, reeds, or anything stiff which could support the weight of petticoats and an over-skirt. Instead of a "handbag" or "purse", side slits allowed a woman to reach into a **pocket**, which was a pouch connected to a waistband. The wide hip design of the pannier-cage allowed for large pockets which could hold a smaller purse of heavy coins, keys, mirror, or anything else. Around the 1780's the silhouette became smaller.

Pennsylvanischer Staatsbote: This is German for "Pennslyvania State Messenger", a weekly newspaper written for the German speakers who moved to the Colonies.

It was designed to inform them about events. Heinrich Miller, a German-born entrepreneur who had made the Colonies his new home, reported on July 5, 1776 the decision of the Continental Congress to vote for the Declaration of Independence from the King of England.

A few days later, the entire Declaration was translated into German and published. The English version of the Declaration of Independence was published on July 4th, 1776 for the members of Congress. The American public could read about it on July 6th.

Perplexed: Confused. Puzzled.

Perturbed: Upset, worried, troubled.

Pliney the Elder - This man was born in Como, Italy around 23 years before Christ was born.He was a scholar and served as a naval and army commander when Emperor Vespasian ruled the Roman Empire. His full name was Gaius Plinius Secundus. He studied plants and developed comprehensive reference books of medicinal recipes, which some think was the seed of the pharmaceutical industry and the concept of an encyclopedia of knowledge. It is said one of his suggestions to alleviate headaches was to take pure rose petals from the Apothecary Rose, steeped in wine for a few weeks. If the mixture was warmed, it could be used as ear drops. A sleepless patient could be given a mixture of rose, mint and cloves to inhale.

Political: A person or group that controls or wants to control the government.

Portray/ portrayal: To describe. To represent. To act on stage.

Posthumously: This is an action which occurs after a person has died....

Primo Uomo This is an Italian term for the

words "First Man". Often in opera, a female star is called the Prima Donna, or the First Lady. The back up would be Seconda Donna or the backup man would be Secondo Uomo. These are terms to reference status on the stage.

Quaint: Charming in an old fashioned way.

Reciprocate: To share the same feelings. When someone gives you a gift, you give a gift in return.

Reconcile: To be friends again. To find a way for two opposite ideas to agree.

Repute: Public respect. Good name. Reputation.

Rig / Rigged/ Rigging: Placement of sails and

masts of a ship.

Satire: A literary genre. A style of writing in which human foolishness is laughed at, often with sarcasm.

Scribe: This was a job function. A person who acted as a scribe copied manuscripts by handwriting them word-for-word. This was before mechanical or electronic devices were invented to make copies. These scribes would also work as the secretary of noble officials, doing such tasks as dictation, bookkeeping, penning and interpreting legal documents, etc. Later this job function transitioned into public professions such as journalist, reporter, etc... This term has been used since the 12th century (1100s).

Self-aggrandizement: When a person boasts or brags and tries to increase his or her own power or wealth.

Sentimental: Showing affectionate gentle, feelings, as in a play onstage.

Sitting-room- The term "sitting" was used

around 1706 to reference a time where one sits, as if being a model while your portrait is being painted. The term "sitting room" was first recorded in 1771. Today, we may call that a living room, or a room with chairs and sofas where guests may sit and chat.

Sons Of Liberty- This is a group of merchants who united to oppose the Stamp Act of 1765. Nightly, they marched in protest in New York City, demanding liberty.

These protests encouraged others to boycott British imported goods. Other people who did not belong to the group started to adopt the term "Sons of Liberty".

These were tenants living on the Hudson River, which is north of New York City. These tenants refused to pay rent, and also refused to vacate the abodes they were renting.

The original Sons of Liberty clarified that these actions were not honorable and these rebellions would not be tolerated by their original Sons of Liberty group who wanted freedom from kings.

The copy-sons of liberty were soon suppressed by British troops and others. Some members of the original group included Isaac Sears, John Lamb, and Alexander McDougall.

Spinning Jenny This was an invention by James Hargraves to make the spinning of fibers for weaving cloth more efficient. The design was also modified by Thomas High.

Statuesque: Tall and beautiful.

Stays - Another term could be "boning" or "corset". This was an undergarment used by ladies which was placed over a chemise and around the torso. Usually, it encased whalebone in fabric pockets to create a conical wrapping around the rib-cage, to cover the torso, then secured with laces. This caused the posture to be very upright.

succinct: Clearly said in just a few words with no wasted extra words.

succumb: To give up. To be defeated.

Tether / Tethered: A rope or chain used for keeping an animal restrained as you dismount as from a horse.

Unassuming: Shy, quiet, modest.

Unobtrusive: Not noticed. Quiet. Shy.

Vague: This is a term meaning uncertain about the specifics. Middle French (around 1540) defines it as empty or vacant or wandering. The Latin term vagas means rambling, vacillating, or uncertain,"

Vexing Means to frustrate to the point of being distressingly annoying or worrisome to that person

.

Volatile: Can change quickly, suddenly

Whine: To make a high, unhappy cry or sound.

146

17 ISBN List for All *Firebrand* Books

This section shall list out all the the ISBN-13 codes which are used to identify each *Firebrand* volume when cataloging books in bookstores and libraries. Use this ISBN to request a volume if your local bookstore or library does not have it in stock.

Firebrand Vol 1	978-1-7184-0013-9
Firebrand Vol 2	978-1-7184-0014-6
Firebrand Vol 3	978-1-7184-0015-3
Firebrand Vol 4	978-1-7184-0016-0
Firebrand Vol 5	978-1-7184-0017-7
Firebrand Vol 6	978-1-7184-0018-4
Firebrand Vol 7	978-1-7184-0019-1
Firebrand Vol 8	978-1-7184-0020-7
Firebrand Vol 9	978-1-7184-0021-4
Firebrand Vol 10	978-1-7184-0022-1
Firebrand Vol 11	978-1-7184-0023-8
Firebrand Vol 12	978-1-7184-0024-5
Firebrand Vol 13	978-1-7184-0025-2
Firebrand Vol 14	978-1-7184-0026-9
Firebrand Vol 15	978-1-7184-0027-6

Firebrand Vol 16-Conversation Station   978-1-7184-0028-3

Firebrand Bundle (16 books shrink-wrapped)978-1-7184-0029-0

18 Ancestry and Descendants

How do the characters in Firebrand relate to the characters in Edges? Below is a simple diagram showing the ancestors:

Man 1700s	Woman 1700s	Descendant 2030's
Button Gwinette	Polly Mulhoolin	→ Bjorn Esterday, Investigative Reporter
Bryce Aiden Tyler	Jane Hargreaves	→ Sarah Paradise, Teacher
Billy Dawes	Silversmith	→ Earth Farmer Community

Magistrate Karl Pinkney	Eliza Lucas	→ Sammy Scribe, Editor of *Daily Memo* Newspaper in Courtly City
Irish Sailor Patrick Scriobhai	Susanna Wright	→ Mrs. Libris, Courtly City librarian
Witherspoon	Grand Estate Cook	→ Queenie Courtly, Originally from AromaX and married to Jack Courtly, ruling couple of Courtly City.

Clergy Pastor at the Church	Polly's Mother

→ Polly is the descendant from her mother, but this new union between the clergy and Polly's widowed mother did not result in more descendants...

they simply lived happily ever after together...

Polly's mother did start the tradition of Courtly City's Widow's Cloisters.

Man from the Wolf Tribe	Marguerite Kanenstenhawi Arosen, of the Bear tribe - As a girl, she was given the name of *A'ongonte* or *Wa'ongote.* This is translated to mean "person who has been replanted" or "one who is planted like an Ash tree" *Kanata.* Is the Iroquois word.for "village settlement". Eunice is her English name. Marguerite is her French Catholic name. When she became an adult, she adopted the name of *Kanenstenhawi,* which means "She who brings in corn"

→ This marriage resulted in TallMan. TallMan may have produced a descendant in the city of AromaX in the 2030's.

AromaX and Courtly City are allies in the decade of 2030.

In 2030

Solve the murder for which you have been blamed.
Observe those in the uniformed squad,
As the class separations they maintain.
Expose the charlatan as a fraud.
Gallantly defend the honor of the slain who
shed blood to free you even-though you're flawed
Travel the path other's dare not deign.
Embrace your destiny despite the odds.
Know propaganda is a miasma
Which may cause us all some strain.

.

About the Author

Wynter Sommers is the pseudonym for an American writing team. The team consists of technology specialists, PhD's, and other field-tested experts.

With over thirty years of in-classroom experience, the authors artistically weave subtle meaning into each narrative to lend lasting appeal to this new classic, which encourages repeated readings.

By reading an enjoyable fictional adventure, the reader learns many educational topics and hones their skills in US History, reading comprehension, critical thinking, social studies and more.

Each time a story theme is explored, new meaning is revealed. Objective facts in the "Did you know" section stimulate conversation, provoking heartfelt introspection on various topics. Everyday Characters in extraordinary situations, demonstrate the value of choosing a real-life action of peace, honor, integrity, truth, patience and perseverance to overcome obstacles in real life. Wynter Sommers hopes each tale inspires action, creativity, and kindness towards your neighbor. One never knows when a small choice today will impact generations into the future.

Choose wisely. True love is the most durable substance on earth. Wynter Sommers hopes you will enjoy the other BJORN ESTERDAY stories.

www.ingramcontent.com/pod-product-compliance
Lightning Source LLC
Chambersburg PA
CBHW030036030726
47500CB00001B/126